Rae stuck her head under the motel room's bed. Just a little clear piece of plastic, but she might as well check it out. She stretched out her hand, straining until she felt the muscles in her back cramp. Then one finger brushed up against the cool, slick surface.

/killed her mother/

The thought ignited her finger as if it was the tip of a long fuse, a fuse that ran up her arm and deep into her chest. Rae ran her finger across the piece of plastic again.

/killed her mother/

The flavor of the thought was a little familiar. The inside of Rae's head itched as she struggled to pinpoint who it reminded her of. "Who is it?" she muttered. "Who?" And finally it came to her. And it was no surprise—the thought felt like it came from the fake meter reader, one of the men who held her prisoner.

Rae couldn't stop herself from touching the piece of plastic again. The spark that had started on her finger traveled farther up the fuse.

/killed her mother/

My mother? she wondered. *Did that man kill my mother?*

The spark reached her chest. And Rae's heart exploded.

Don't miss any of the books in this
thrilling new series:

fingerprints

fingerprints

betrayed

melinda metz

AVON BOOKS
An Imprint of HarperCollins*Publishers*

Betrayed

Printed in the United States of America.

For information address
HarperCollins Children's Books, a division of
HarperCollins Publishers, 1350 Avenue of the Americas,
New York, NY 10019.

 Produced by 17th Street Productions,
an Alloy Online, Inc. company
33 West 17th Street, New York, NY 10011

Library of Congress Catalog Card Number: 00-193288
ISBN 0-06-447282-5

First Avon edition, 2001

Visit us on the World Wide Web!
www.harperteen.com

For Julia Richardson,
third member of Team Fingerprints, with many thanks
from Melinda and Liesa.

betrayed

Chapter 1

Rae Voight closed her eyes. She felt her body sink down into her soft bed. Deeper, deeper, her breath becoming deeper, too. Slower. Then her right leg kicked out. Her head jerked back. And her eyes snapped open. "You're not there anymore," she whispered, hoping saying the words out loud would help her believe them. "You're home. You're safe."

Safe. But for how long? The men who had held her and Yana captive in the Motel 6 hadn't found out whatever it was they wanted to know. Whoever they were, they weren't finished with her. Rae didn't think they'd be finished until she was dead. Or they were.

Rae's eyes began to itch. She needed to blink, but she didn't want to shut her eyes again, even for a fraction of a second. If she did, it would happen.

She'd be back in the Motel 6, tied up, helpless. The itching increased. Rae had to blink. Had to. She flicked her eyelids down—and saw herself on the floor of the motel room. She could actually feel the thick, nubby blindfold pressing against her eyes, even though her eyelids had already flicked back up.

Light. She needed light. Rae sat up in bed and switched on the lamp on her nightstand. There was no way she was ever getting to sleep, not when closing her eyes long enough to blink freaked her out. She glanced at her alarm clock—a little after 4 A.M. Thank God. She could get up in another hour or so without her dad going into parental concern overdrive. Rae blinked as fast as she could. Having the light on definitely helped somehow, even during a blink.

A plan. I need some kind of plan, she thought. But her brain was blank, like a fried computer. *Okay, so I'll get Yana and Anthony to help. Maybe even Jesse. I'll ask them all to meet up here after—*

Rae's heart went still, then gave a hard double thump. Someone was in the hall. They were trying to be quiet, but she knew they were there. What if it was him—her kidnapper? The non–meter reader. The man she'd been so close to without knowing what he was capable of, what he would soon do to her. She heard the whisper of cloth—a sleeve? a pant leg?—against the wall. And there—just then—the soft creak of a floorboard. Rae knew that board. It was the loose one about three steps from her bedroom door. Whoever was out there was close. Very close. She jerked her eyes to the window. Closed. Locked. There wouldn't be time to—

A faint squeak interrupted her thoughts. Rae whipped her head back toward the door, her eyes riveted on the doorknob, the turning doorknob. She opened her mouth to scream—and her father stepped into the room.

"Dad," Rae exclaimed, the word coming out cracked from her dry throat.

"I saw your light. I was up to use the bathroom," he said, jamming his hands in the deep pockets of his worn terry cloth robe.

"I was, um, studying. History test tomorrow," Rae explained, realizing a moment too late that she had no book out, no notebook, nothing.

"Actually, I was lying," her father told her. "I couldn't sleep."

"Me, neither," Rae admitted. She scooted closer to the headboard so she could lean against it.

Her father sat down on the edge of the bed. "I kept replaying all the things I said to you when you got home from the concert. I was too harsh. I—"

"No. You were right. It was completely wrong of me just to call and announce I was crashing after the concert and wouldn't be home until morning." Rae didn't tell him she'd been forced by her kidnappers to tell him that lie. If her dad knew what really happened Saturday night, he'd never let her out of his sight again. And he'd probably give himself an ulcer. She remembered how he'd looked when he used to come visit her in the hospital after her breakdown. He'd looked like he should be in the hospital himself, his skin all gray, his clothes loose from the weight he'd lost. Rae never wanted to see him like that again. Especially not because of her.

"Ever since . . . summer," her father began. Rae knew he really meant ever since she'd been put in the mental hospital. "Ever since then, I know I've been a pain." A burst of laughter escaped Rae. That was so not what she was expecting her dad to say. "Buying you that cell phone so I could always check up on you," he continued. "And remember how I wanted to get a live-in housekeeper?" he asked.

"Yeah. I remember," Rae told him. It had taken her at least a week to talk him out of that one.

"I want you to know that it's not that I don't trust you. You have more sense than most of my college students," her dad said. He rubbed the bump on his nose, the bump that Rae had inherited. "It's just that even when you're my age, I'm probably going to feel like it's my job to keep you safe. Last summer—no,

4

last spring, last fall, or even before that, I should have seen—"

"No," Rae cut him off. "It—it wasn't like that. It happened really fast. There was nothing for you to see." That was the truth. Rae's fingerprint-reading power had appeared like a light switch being turned on. At first she'd thought she was going nuts, that she was hearing voices in her head like a psycho killer. Then she'd realized—well, Anthony Fascinelli had realized—what was really going on. When Rae touched a fingerprint, she got the thought the person who'd left the print was having. "And I'm okay now. I really am," she added.

"I guess we should both get a little sleep," her father answered. He clicked off her lamp. "Next time you want to stay over somewhere after a concert or something, ask first. I'll probably manage to give permission for you to be out of my sight for that long."

"I will," Rae said as he headed out. He shut the door behind him, returning the room to full darkness. Rae realized she'd been blinking away during their whole conversation with no trauma flashes.

So I just need to keep myself distracted, she thought. There was only one thing she could think of that had the power to occupy every molecule of her brain now that she was alone in the dark again—that kiss. That body-melting kiss between her and Anthony after he found her at the motel, found her and carried her to safety.

Experimentally Rae closed her eyes, trying to remember every detail. One of his hands had been twined in her hair, his fingers grazing the back of her neck. That one touch had been enough to send lava down her body. But Anthony'd had one hand under her shirt, on her bare back. And his mouth . . . God. She'd never felt anything like it. Never. It was like she'd walked around her whole life with her body set on six and Anthony had cranked it up to ten. Heat began pumping through Rae again just thinking about it.

I'm never falling asleep now, she thought. But she didn't care. This was worth staying awake for. Rae replayed the kiss over and over, and it only gained in intensity. When her clock radio began to play, she could hardly believe that hours had passed. Had she actually fallen asleep? If she had, a dream had started exactly where her imagination had left off. She'd spent every moment with Anthony, awake or asleep. She was certain of that.

What am I going to wear? The thought had her out of bed and on her feet in seconds. She rushed over to the closet, yanked it open, and studied the contents. *Like Anthony actually notices what you wear,* she thought.

Except that he probably did, in that guy way. Maybe he wouldn't be able to say what she'd had on a minute after she was out of his sight, but he'd have an impression—sexy or girlie or something.

Rae ran her finger along the row of clothes. She stopped on her suede skirt, the short one. Anthony liked to look at her in that. She'd seen it on his face. Maybe he couldn't say the color or what it was made of, but it was one of his favorites. Rae picked out a light blue cashmere sweater set to go with it and a pair of flats. She didn't mind it when her heels made her taller than Anthony was, but she was pretty sure he hated it.

After she carefully laid out her clothes on the bed, ignoring the soft buzz of her own old thoughts, Rae hurried to the bathroom. She wanted time to do the hair mud pack and give her legs a quick shave so she could wear the skirt.

Rae only stepped out of the shower when the water turned cold. She knew her father would give her grief for hogging the hot water—he was always saying it should be absolutely impossible for the two of them to come close to using all the water in the reservoir of the hot water heater. But Rae didn't care. In a little more than an hour, she'd be seeing Anthony. Yeah, it was true that she saw him all the time. But that kiss—that kiss had changed everything. It had for

7

her, at least. And from the way he'd acted as he drove her home early Sunday morning after dropping off Jesse and Yana—so quiet and serious—she was pretty sure Anthony felt the same way.

What am I going to say to him? she wondered as she started to dry her hair. *Do I mention the kiss—no. That would be lame. But am I supposed to just act like nothing is different? Just say hi—and oh, yeah, thanks for saving my life—then head off to my locker?*

What am I going to say to him? Rae was still wondering as she headed toward the main entrance of Sanderson Prep an hour later. She scanned the crowd, and her heart slammed against her ribs as she spotted Anthony leaning against the railing of the front steps. For an instant she felt like she was in his arms again, being carried out of the motel. She could actually feel the heat of his body.

Was that fake meter reader kidnapper watching me and Anthony in the motel parking lot Saturday night? she thought. *Is he already making a new plan to get whatever it is he wants from me?*

And then kill me, she couldn't stop herself from adding.

You're coming up with a plan, too, she reminded herself. *You and Anthony, and Yana and Jesse.* She took one step toward Anthony, then someone grabbed her by the elbow. Rae jerked away.

"Sorry. Did I scare you?" Marcus Salkow asked.

Rae let out a short breath. "A little. I didn't see you come up," she said. And she wished he hadn't. She wanted to get over to Anthony. Right now.

Marcus shifted awkwardly from foot to foot, which was so not the usual Marcus Salkow, school demigod. *Is he going to ask me out again?* Rae wondered. *Is he going to try and convince me to take him back right here and now?*

"I got this for you." Marcus pulled a long velvet box out of his football jacket and thrust it at her. "It's to say I'm sorry—for what a jerk I was when you were in the hospital. I know it really hurt you. Me getting together with Dori without telling you and everything."

"You didn't have to." Rae didn't open the box. "You already apologized, and—"

"It's not just for that," Marcus interrupted. He clicked his teeth together nervously. "It's to show you that, you know, I really care about you. No matter what. Whether you ever end up wanting to be with me or not."

Rae stared down at the box, trying to decide what to say. There were too many emotions rushing around inside her, anger and affection and sadness.

"Open it," Marcus said softly.

Slowly Rae raised the lid and saw a tennis

bracelet cradled on the box's satin lining. The sunlight caught on the diamonds, turning them into white fire. *Diamonds*. What was she supposed to do?

Rae. The moment Anthony saw her, it was like his body had a flashback. He could feel her lips against his. He could feel her arms around his neck. Instantly he was moving toward her. It took three steps for his brain to register what she was holding in her hand. It was that bracelet, that freaking diamond bracelet, the one Salkow had bought for her.

Anthony forced his eyes away from Rae, and, yeah, there was Salkow standing next to her with a crazy grin on his face. Why wouldn't he look happy after handing Rae a present like that? Salkow had acted all worried about whether or not she'd like it—he'd even shown it to Anthony to see what Anthony thought. As if there was any question that any girl anywhere wouldn't get all ecstatic at the sight of it.

He turned away and started back up to the main doors. What in the hell had he been thinking kissing Rae when he knew for a fact Salkow was getting back together with her? She deserved a guy like that, a guy who could—

"Anthony, wait a minute." Anthony's heart shot up into his throat, and his stomach lurched up into the empty space in his chest. Rae'd come after him.

He turned to face her—but saw Jackie Kane standing there. His organs slithered back into place.

"You're out of the hospital," he said. A total moron comment.

"My parents wanted me to stay home for a few days, but I wanted to come back right away. Less gossip time," Jackie explained. "If I'm here, no one can say I died from my aspirin OD or that I'm in a designer straitjacket somewhere."

Anthony nodded. *Is this girl—this quiet, all-buttoned-up girl—the real Jackie?* he wondered. She was nothing like the girl who'd been chugging vodka at McHugh's party last week. Absolutely nothing like the girl who'd shoved him against the wall and kissed him until he could hardly stay on his feet.

"I wanted you to know—" Jackie took a quick glance over her shoulder. "My parents and I have our first family counseling meeting on Wednesday. In a few weeks my brother, Phillip, is going to come to one of the meetings, too."

Good, Anthony thought. From what Jackie had told him, make that what he'd pried out of her, Phillip was a big part of the problem in her family. "Was it hard to get them to say they'd do it?" Anthony asked.

"The . . . my suicide attempt scared them more than I thought it would. When the doctor told them

I'd said I wanted family counseling, they fell all over themselves getting out a credit card and signing us up." Jackie gave a small smile. "I think they decided counseling would be a lot less embarrassing than whatever I'd do next. And all the best people see therapists," she added, more than a little sarcasm creeping into her voice.

"If you ever want to talk about any of it, you know, with a nonprofessional, I'm around," Anthony said. He noticed one of the laces on his sneakers was loose, and he bent down to retie it.

"Thanks," Jackie said.

Anthony retied the lace of his other shoe, even though it wasn't loose, then shoved himself to his feet. "I should go hit my locker."

"Okay," Jackie said quickly. She smoothed a stray section of her blond hair into her ponytail. "But first let me apologize for—" She hesitated. "For what I did to you at the party. I was—"

"In a vodka haze," Anthony finished for her, wanting to get this conversation done with.

"Well, yeah," Jackie admitted. "I was doing every stupid thing I could think of, like you said in the hospital, to get my parents to notice me. God, you saw me shoplifting and driving drunk—" Jackie stopped abruptly. Her cheeks turned pink. "I didn't mean kissing you was like those things."

Anthony knew kissing him was definitely on the list of stupid crap she'd done, but he didn't call her on it.

"It's just not something I'd usually do," Jackie rushed on. "At least not so fast," she added, speaking so quickly, the words came out jumbled together.

Message received, Anthony thought. *I get that there's no chance in hell anything's going to happen between us.* The first bell rang. "I gotta go," Anthony said, for once actually happy classes were about to start. "See you." He hurried to the main doors.

"Bye," Jackie called after him. "And thanks again."

Anthony gave a little hand flip, not wanting to turn back and be forced to look at her, then he pushed his way through the doors and strode down the hall. He got smiles and "hi's" from a couple of girls—more than a couple. But that's because he was good on the football field. That's the only reason they'd let him into Sanderson Prep in the first place.

None of the smiles meant anything more than "that's the guy who won us the game." They weren't invitations or anything. *So is it finally through your thick head?* he asked himself. *Jackie made out with you because she wanted to be a bad girl. Rae kissed you because you saved her life.* It didn't mean anything. *Rae—make that Rae, Jackie, and every girl in this friggin' school—wants to end up with a guy like Salkow. A guy who belongs.*

Rae hurried out the back doors and immediately scanned the parking lot for Anthony's mom's Hyundai. She knew he always dropped his mom off at work so he could have the car until it was time to pick her up.

Good, it's still there, she thought. *It should be.* She'd sprinted out here—well, the Rae version of sprinting, which wasn't all *that* fast—after the last bell. She couldn't go the rest of the day without seeing him.

Was he avoiding her? Was that why he hadn't shown up in the caf? *If he is, it's because of that bracelet. He saw Marcus give it to me. I know it. And he went inside before he could see me give it back.* God, who knew what was going on in Anthony's head right now?

Rae decided to stake out his car. It was the only way she'd be absolutely sure he wouldn't slip by her. She started across the lot and spotted Yana Savari's bright yellow VW Bug. Perfect. She and Yana could keep watch for Anthony together while Rae told Yana about the bracelet and how Anthony'd stayed out of sight all day. Yana'd help her analyze the sitch. It was part of best-friend duty.

Before Rae could reach the car, Yana climbed out. One look at Yana's face and all thoughts of Anthony slid out of Rae's head. She rushed over to her friend. "What's wrong?" she exclaimed. "Did the guys from the motel come after you again? Did—"

"You know exactly what's wrong," Yana snapped. "Don't pretend you don't." Her blue eyes were bright with anger, and her face was flushed.

"What?" Rae cried.

"What?" Yana repeated, her lips curling into a sneer. "I can't believe you're asking me what. Are you going to try and pretend that you didn't know what I told you in the motel was a secret?"

"What?" Rae hadn't meant to say the word again, but she had no idea what Yana was talking about. "Of course I knew," she added quickly.

"You knew, but it didn't mean a thing to you. You had to be Little Miss Do-good and try to fix things. Just like you did when you went looking for Anthony's dad. Didn't that smack any sense into your head? You don't know anything about his life. And you absolutely don't know anything about mine," Yana spat out.

Rae forced herself to meet Yana's gaze, even though the fury radiating out of her light blue eyes was so powerful that Rae could almost feel her skin singeing. "Back up, okay? Just tell me—"

Yana shook her head, her bleached blond hair flying around her face. "Oh, I get it. You're going to pretend that you don't know anything about the letter." She moved closer, going almost nose to nose with Rae. "Did you think because you didn't sign it, I'd be too stupid to figure out who it was from? I only told one person about my seventh birthday and the ballet—you."

Rae stayed exactly where she was, fighting the urge to back away. "I still don't know what you're talking about," she said, forcing herself to speak the words softly and calmly. "What letter?"

"The letter to my dad. The one that told him how much his—what was the word you used?—oh, yeah, *indifference,* you said how much his *indifference* had hurt me. Then you told the whole ballet story. Not that I wouldn't have figured out it was you who sent it, anyway. It was so you, Rae."

Yana started to turn away. Rae reached out and caught her arm. "I didn't do it. You have to believe me. We thought we might be being monitored in the motel, remember?"

"Oh, right. And one of the men who kidnapped us felt so sorry for me that he decided to write a letter to my father." Yana jerked her arm free. "Just stay out of my life from now on."

"You don't—"

"Get away from me," Yana yelled. "Now!"

Rae felt tears sting her eyes, and she was suddenly aware that she and Yana were drawing a crowd. "Fine," Rae answered. Clearly it wouldn't help to talk to Yana right now. If it would, Rae wouldn't care how many people were watching. But it was pointless.

She turned and walked into the school building, then headed for the closest bathroom. Once inside she locked herself in a stall. The moment the metal bar slid into place, the tears started streaking down her face, hot against her skin. Rae pressed the heels of her hands against her mouth, pushing her lips hard against her teeth. She couldn't keep herself from crying, but she wasn't going to let anyone else hear her.

Yana was her best friend. How could she believe Rae would lie to her face? Rae yanked a handful of toilet paper squares out of the metal dispenser, then wiped her eyes viciously.

Enough, she thought. *Crying isn't going to fix things with Yana. I need to prove to her that I didn't send the letter. And that means showing her exactly who did.*

The only ones it could be were the men who had held her and Yana in the motel. She'd thought they might be listening to her and Yana, even though they'd been left alone in the room. Now she'd just have to prove it.

Rae threw the soggy toilet paper into the toilet and flushed. They—the men—had to have sent the letter to Yana as a way to get to Rae. Had they figured out how Yana would react? Had they been trying to make Yana think Rae had betrayed her?

It made sense in a twisted way, Rae thought. They knew Yana had gone to the motel to help Rae. So they'd torn Yana away from her. *They want me alone. That's what it is,* she decided. *They want me helpless.*

Well, that's not going to happen.

Chapter 2

Anthony hurled himself at the tackle dummy, sending it lurching backward. He retreated a few steps and flung himself at it again.

"Save something for the game, Fascinelli," Coach Mosier yelled. Anthony nodded—then rammed his body into the dummy as hard as he could. He didn't want to save anything. He wanted the sweat. The crunch. The pain. It was the only thing that kept his mind off—the only thing that kept his mind where it should be.

Anthony battered the dummy, grunting as he charged it again and again. "Whoo-hoo! Go, Anthony," someone called from the stands. Anthony wiped the sweat out of his eyes and glanced in the direction the voice had come from. Yana. He felt like he'd just taken a hit to the belly. If Yana was here, that had to mean Rae was, too. He'd spent lunch pumping iron so he wouldn't have to deal with her, and now she was here. He pulled in a gulp of the grass-scented air and scanned the stands. He couldn't stop himself. No Rae.

Okay, good, good. Anthony lowered his shoulder and slammed the dummy again, welcoming the spike of pain stabbing into his arm. *Focus on that,* he thought.

"Showers," the coach yelled.

Anthony wasn't ready to stop. *Do some laps,* he ordered himself, and immediately started around the field. Yeah, he'd run until he collapsed somewhere. Because that's what it would take to stop thinking about her. And he had to stop thinking about her or he'd go nuts. *Diamond bracelet, remember?* he asked himself.

Why had he kissed her? If he hadn't, it would be so much easier—

"Fascinelli, what are you doing?" Coach Mosier called.

"Just some laps," he shouted back without breaking stride.

"I say when you do laps," the coach answered. "And I say when you shower. Locker room—now!"

Anthony reluctantly slowed to a walk, the muscles

in his thighs and calves on fire, and turned toward the gym. A moment later he felt someone tap his shoulder. "No time for your adoring public?" Yana asked as she fell into step beside him.

"Where's Rae?" The words just came ripping out, like a burp after chugging a big gulp of Coke. "You meeting her here or something?"

"Oh, I've already seen Rae," Yana answered. "And I'm hoping I never see her again."

"Huh?" There was still too much blood slamming around in Anthony's brain from practice. He wasn't getting her.

"Rae's still acting like the little rich girl who has to save all us commoners from our horrible little lives," Yana told him, her blue eyes narrowed into slits. "I just thought you might want to know that."

"What?" Anthony kept walking. This wasn't a conversation he wanted to be having. Just talking about Rae kept giving him flashes of that kiss.

"She wrote a letter to my dad saying that he wasn't treating me right. Can you believe that?" Yana demanded. "I mean, did she not learn anything from the fiasco of finding your dad in, you know?"

In prison, Anthony silently finished for her. He ran his fingers through his damp hair. "She was just trying to—"

"You're not going to defend her, are you?" Yana

interrupted. "Don't bother. I know exactly how pissed off at her you were. I was there, remember?"

"Yeah," Anthony said. What did Yana want from him? Had she sat through practice just so she could rant about Rae? "Look, I gotta go in," he told her when they reached the door to the locker room.

"You want to meet up later?" Yana asked abruptly. "Go dancing or something? I swear, if I don't do something active, I'm going to human combust. Every time I think about what she did, I just—" Yana let out a shrill shriek.

Anthony frowned. Didn't she have any other friends? Or a boyfriend, even? She seemed like the kind of girl who'd have a bunch of guys she could snap her fingers at whenever she wanted one.

"I'm not really a dancing—" Anthony began.

"You were fine in New Orleans," Yana said. "And I hate going out by myself. I don't want any slimeballs hitting on me. I just want to dance."

Anthony shook his head. "I have to—" *What?* he asked himself. *Go home, deal with the rug rats, and, uh, try not to think about Rae.*

"It's not just the Rae thing," Yana added when Anthony didn't finish. "My dad basically told me he wants me out of the house until late. Some hot date with some flavor of the hour. Like I'd want to be there to witness that."

Anthony understood that. Big time. His mother had dragged home quite a few semihuman specimens. Anthony'd spent many a late night taking the kids to movies or McDonald's to get them out of the way. He felt a twinge of sympathy for Yana. Maybe she was asking him because she knew he'd get it and her other friends wouldn't.

"Sure. Why not? Where do you want me to meet you?" he asked.

"Club 112 at nine," Yana told him.

"Okay. See you there." Anthony headed into the locker room and stripped when he reached his locker.

"Who's the girl?" Sanders yelled as soon as Anthony stepped into the steamy shower room.

"Nobody," Anthony answered. He tilted back his head and let the water pound his face.

"You're not getting out of this. We all saw her," McHugh said. "Is she from your old school? Does she have a friend? Because I heard some very interesting things about Fillmore girls that I'd like to check out for myself. I mean, they're supposed to be wild, right?"

"Very nice, McHugh," Marcus commented. "So *do* you have something going with her?" he asked Anthony.

"Yeah." The word just popped out of Anthony's

mouth. Why not let Marcus think he was with Yana? It would make it easier to leave Rae alone. Until she and Salkow got back together. Because they would. Everyone at school knew it.

Rae got off the bus and started down the block. Her heart began fluttering in her chest when the Motel 6 came into sight. *They're not still there,* she told herself. But the frantic beating of her heart didn't slow down.

Reluctantly she climbed the outdoor staircase to the second floor, the same staircase Anthony had carried her down. *He would have come with me,* she thought. *Even if he's avoiding me, he wouldn't have wanted me to come here by myself.*

They're not here anymore, she told herself again. *You don't need Anthony for protection.* And besides, after that scene with Yana, Rae had wanted to be alone. Now that she was actually here, she wanted that a lot less. *But the men aren't here anymore,* she thought again.

But where are they? she couldn't help wondering. She snorted. Maybe the first question she should be asking was *who* were they. She knew who one of them was. Well, not really. She knew one of them had gotten into her backyard posing as a meter reader. She'd even talked to the guy—which was why she recognized his voice when he had her tied up in the motel room. But it wasn't like knowing that one of the guys was the fake meter reader did any good. It wasn't like she could give the cops a name or anything.

The woman who had called her and told her to come to the motel said that Aiden wanted to meet her. So there was a slim chance that the other guy was Aiden Matthews, the guy Rae and Yana had run into at the Wilton Community Center when they were trying to get information about Rae's mother. Rae hadn't heard the second man's voice, so she couldn't be sure if he was Aiden or not.

But it just didn't make sense. She hadn't gotten the sense that Aiden would be capable of something like that. And besides, when you were going to kidnap someone, you didn't announce who you were.

Rae froze. *Unless you planned to kill the person you kidnapped. Then it wouldn't matter.* God, was the other guy Aiden? What did he know about her mother? From touching his fingertips that day at the center, Rae had picked up the fact that Aiden knew her mother had been experimented on. Had he actually seen the experiments? Had he done them? Had he tried to help Rae's mother? Was he so freaked out that Rae would find out the truth about what happened to her mother and the other women in her

New Agey group that he was willing to kill Rae?

Rae's heartbeat accelerated until it was beating as fast as a hummingbird's wings. "One thing at a time," she whispered, taking a little comfort in the sound of her own voice. "You're here to check the room. Think about the rest later." She climbed the last few steps and shoved on the metal bar that opened the door. She didn't pick up a single thought. So not a single print. Which was weird. The Motel 6 wasn't the kind of place they cleaned to the point of spotlessness.

But maybe I just hit the day of their monthly supercleaning, Rae thought. *It doesn't have to mean that somebody—like the fake meter reader or Aiden—came back and cleared the place of any evidence.*

Rae made her way down the hall and stopped in front of room 212. Her head felt weightless, like it had turned into a helium balloon, and she swayed on her feet. *Don't lose it,* she ordered herself. *This is not a place you want to end up fainting.*

She gave her head a hard shake, and some of the strange balloon-brain sensation disappeared. *Okay, probably not much point in checking 212,* she decided. The guys probably wore gloves in there. She might have better luck in the room across the hall, the room where she'd been taken to go to the bathroom. The men might have been more careless in their room. If they left a few prints, Rae could end up with some valuable info.

So the first thing I need to do—duh—is get inside the room. Rae spotted a cleaning cart near the end of the hall and trotted toward it. The door closest to the cart stood ajar, and Rae poked her head in. "Uh, hi," she said to the cleaning woman. "I was in room 213 last night, and I think I left my notebook in there. Do you think maybe I could—" Rae's words trailed off. The cleaning woman was just staring at her, face expressionless. Rae felt like she'd have more luck talking to the wall. "It would just take a minute," she added. The woman still didn't say anything. What was her problem?

Money. Maybe she wants money. Rae fumbled for her purse, letting her old thoughts rush through her mind without focusing on them, managed to unzip it, and pulled a twenty out of her wallet. She dropped it as she tried to hand it to the woman. "Sorry," Rae muttered. She reached for the twenty, but the woman was faster. She had the bill in her pocket before Rae's fingers were halfway to it.

"Come on," the woman said. Without another word, she led the way down to room 213 and unlocked the door. "Don't take all day about it," she told Rae, then headed back toward her cart.

Rae ducked into the room and closed the door. She got nothing off the doorknob, and the air was thick with the smell of disinfectant. *Doesn't mean there isn't a print they missed,* Rae told herself. She started her search with the dresser, running her fingers over every inch. Nothing. Her fingertips ended up coated with oily furniture polish, so she headed into the bathroom and washed her hands, then continued the search. Medicine cabinet. Nothing. Hot and cold water taps. Nothing. Towel rack. Nothing. Toilet handle. Nothing. Little window. Nothing. Water glasses—clearly fresh with their little accordion-pleated paper tops.

Okay, okay, back to the main room. TV remote. Nothing. Phone. Nothing. Phone book. Nothing. The cleaning woman wouldn't have wiped down the phone book. Clearly somebody else had gone over the place. *And gee, I wonder who?* she thought.

Headboards on the two double beds. Nothing. Thermostat, nothing. Nightstand. Nothing. Bible. Nothing.

What else? What else? Rae surveyed the room. What had she missed? Her eyes darted back and forth, searching, searching. *I know!* she thought. *The little plastic thing on the end of the curtain pull.* She rushed over and ran her fingers over it. Nothing. *Gotta be something else,* she thought.

Light switches! Everybody touched those. Nothing. Nothing. Nothing.

Rae tried the bedspreads, even though the strong scent of detergent made it seem unlikely she'd find anything. And she didn't.

All right, I know, or at least I'm pretty sure, that they were listening to me and Yana. So there was probably a bug in our room. And whatever they were using as a receiver, they probably took with them. So that's not helping at all.

Rae checked the wastebasket—empty—then searched it for prints and got, of course—nothing. *What else?* she thought. The closet. With two long steps she reached it. The doorknob was clean. So was the shelf. And the folding thing you could unfold and put your suitcases on. She slowly closed the closet door and studied the room again.

I guess I should look under the beds, she decided. *Just in case.* She walked over to the narrow space between the beds and stretched out on her stomach. The carpet smelled like beer and shampoo and old vomit. Rae covered her nose with one hand and peered under the bed to her left. Nothing. She turned her head to the right. Noth—

Wait. There *was* something there. Something that glistened in the dimness. Rae stuck her head under the bed. Just a little clear piece of plastic, but she might as well check it out. She stretched out her hand, straining until she felt the muscles in her back cramp. Then one finger brushed up against the cool, slick surface.

/killed her mother/

The thought ignited her finger as if it was the tip of a long fuse, a fuse that ran up her arm and deep into her chest. Rae ran her finger across the piece of plastic again.

/killed her mother/

The flavor of the thought was a little familiar. The inside of Rae's head itched as she struggled to pinpoint who it reminded her of. "Who is it?" she muttered. "Who?" And finally it came to her. And it was no surprise—the thought felt like it came from the fake meter reader, one of the men who held her prisoner.

Rae couldn't stop herself from touching the piece of plastic again. The spark that had started on her finger traveled farther up the fuse.

/killed her mother/

My mother? she wondered. *Did that man kill my mother?*

The spark reached her chest. And Rae's heart exploded.

The little dance floor of 112 was packed. Anthony didn't have room to do more than sort of rub up against Yana in time to the music. Which was fine by him. He was a lousy dancer, anyway. And the sensation of Yana's body repeatedly brushing against his— well, it was nice. Although if he was this close to Rae—

Crap. He'd done it again. He was here with Yana so that he wouldn't be sitting home, thinking about Rae until his brains started oozing out of his ears. But every few seconds Rae would appear in his head, and she'd be looking at him the way she had in the Motel 6 parking lot, and he'd be falling again, falling into the blue of her eyes.

"I wonder what Rae and the King of Wonder Bread are doing right now," Yana said, speaking right into his ear so he could hear her over the pounding music.

"Huh?" Anthony mumbled, still halfway submerged in the memory of Rae's eyes.

"You know—Marcus. What do you think he and Rae do for fun?" Yana answered. She threaded her fingers in his belt loops and pulled him even closer. "Go on-line and check their stocks? You know Rae got a lot of money when her mom died, right? Well, at least her dad put it in an account for her."

"Never said anything to me about it," Anthony said, his head filled with an image of Rae, Marcus, and that freakin' bracelet. Was she *thanking* him for it right now, parked in some dark place in his Range Rover, or his BMW—whichever expensive car he was driving today?

"She's embarrassed about it," Yana told him. "At least around people like us. We're probably the only Benjamin-challenged people she's ever hung with."

Why are we talking about Rae? Anthony thought. It was the last thing he wanted. And wasn't the whole point of going out for Yana to blow off steam? She was just getting herself more and more pissed off.

"Probably why she's so gaga over Marcus. They're, like, a perfectly matched set or something," Yana continued.

Okay, so maybe Rae is the second-to-last thing I want to talk about, Anthony thought. The absolute last thing was talking about Rae and Marcus and how perfect they were together.

"So I guess she really loved him?" Anthony asked. Immediately he wished he could rip his tongue out and throw it on the dance floor. Why had he asked that?

"Make that loves," Yana replied. "Whether she admits it or not, Rae's never gotten over him."

"So why aren't they together?" Anthony's demonic tongue made him ask.

"Probably she just wants to make him pay, at least a little longer." Yana wrapped her arms around

Anthony's waist. "God, why do I keep talking about Rae? I'm so pissed at her. She's the last thing I want to be thinking about right now."

Anthony felt her warm breath against his neck, then his ear. His brain turned off. It was like his ear had wires running all the way through his body. He couldn't think about Rae now. He couldn't think about anything. Those wires in his body were sizzling. Frying. Electrocuting him. Maybe he'd never be able to think again.

Then Yana slowly let her face drift closer to his, and her lips pressed against his mouth. The wires running through him snapped. The current stopped flowing. Yeah, he could still feel the heat of her mouth against his, but his brain had flipped back on. And all he could think about was Rae. When he'd kissed her, it had been—

Don't go there, he ordered himself. *No thinking about her.*

Anthony lowered his mouth to the hollow at the base of Yana's throat, tasting sweat and the bitterness of perfume. *Weren't we just supposed to be dancing?* he thought. But this was better. There was no way dancing by itself could get Rae out of his head. Not that the neck kissing was exactly working, either.

Yana pulled him closer, and some of those wires repaired themselves. His brain flickered, but it didn't go blank. Not entirely. Even though he wished it would.

Chapter 3

Rae gently placed the piece of plastic on her nightstand. She'd touched it too many times since she'd gotten home from the Motel 6. It was like a scab. She knew she should stop picking at it, but she couldn't stop.

/killed her mother/

At least it had finally gotten through her brain that the thought couldn't be about her mother. Rae's mom had died in the hospital of that strange wasting disease, the disease that had consumed her body so quickly that the doctors didn't have time to diagnose it.

The disease I might have some mutated version of, Rae thought with a shiver. *Some slow version that gives me numb spots whenever I make a fingertip-to-fingertip connection with someone.*

Not what you should be thinking of when you're about to go to sleep, Rae told herself. She clicked off her lamp and slid under the covers. *Concentrate on whose mother that thought could be about— that's slightly less nightmare inducing.*

There was Mandy Reese. It made some sense that the guy, the fake meter reader, who'd been spying on Rae, would be thinking about Mandy's mom, Amanda. Mandy's mother had been part of the group at the Wilton Center, the group Rae's mother had been in. Two days before the fake meter reader—the FMR—had taken Rae and Yana prisoner, Rae and Yana had been asking a bunch of questions at the center. Rae didn't think that was a coincidence. She figured the FMR was freaked because he thought Rae had gotten close to finding out something. Something about the group. The experiments, whatever they were? Maybe. But definitely something that Rae could have found out at the center. Something about Rae's mother. Which could also mean something about Mandy's mother.

Rae let out a sigh. There were way too many variables. She hated variables. Like that guy Aiden, the one who had given them a two-minute tour of the center. What was his deal? *Was* he the second guy at the motel? Or had the woman—whoever she was—just used Aiden's name because she knew Rae had talked to Aiden?

And God, why wouldn't she know about that? She was working with the FMR, and the FMR had been watching every move Rae made. Anthony's car had been bugged. Rae had been photographed with a telephoto lens.

Rae rolled onto her side and made sure her curtains were closed. They were. But the FMR could be out there, watching, waiting for his next Rae sighting. Waiting to kill her? Possibly.

That's because I got close to something at the center, Rae thought. *Something big. And I'm not going to back away. I want to prove to Yana that I didn't send that letter. And oh, yeah, like I'd ever forget, I want to find out who wants me dead.*

Rae shivered again. She wrapped the covers around herself until they were mummy tight, but she still felt cold.

Because you're scared, she told herself. *The only way to find out what you need to know is to go back to the Wilton Center, and that terrifies you.*

* * *

Kill her. Kill her. Kill her. Kill her! KILL HER!

I want Rae Voight dead. It's all I can think about. There's a voice, a voice that doesn't completely sound like mine, that is always chanting in the back of my head. Kill her! Kill her!

Kill her! Is it my mother's voice? Has some part of her made it back from the dead?

If you're here somewhere, Mom, don't worry. I want revenge as much as you do. You don't have to beg me to kill Rae. I ache to do it.

But I can't. Not yet. Not until I know exactly who else is after Rae. Because they could be after me, too.

So you'll just have to be patient a little longer. We both will. But I swear to you, the instant it's possible, I will put Rae in the ground. And until then, I'll make her suffer in any way I can.

* * *

"So Rae wouldn't take the bracelet." Marcus gave a grunt as he raised the weight he was bench pressing.

"She wouldn't?" Anthony said. He struggled to keep his face expressionless as he stared down at Marcus, spotting him. *She wouldn't?* he repeated to himself. What girl wouldn't snatch up that bracelet in a heartbeat? Did that mean that Rae—

"So now what am I supposed to do?" Marcus asked, jerking Anthony away from his thoughts.

How did I get to be this guy's freakin' romance adviser? Anthony thought, wishing there was anybody else in the weight room who would jump in. "One more set," he told Marcus, avoiding the question.

"It's not like I just threw the bracelet at her,"

Marcus continued. "I knew that wouldn't work. I told her I was sorry about what a jerk I was when she was in the hospital and all that." Marcus thrust the weights over his head.

"Don't lock your elbows," Anthony reminded him. Clearly Marcus was going to spew no matter what. So what Anthony had to do was give him some "uh-huhs" and "yeahs" and attempt to hear the Marcus rant as noise. No words. Just noise.

"So what does she want from me? What else could she possibly want from me?" Marcus's breath came in harsh pants. "I know she, you know, that Rae loved me when we were together. And that can't have changed, not so fast. So what does she want?"

Crap. Anthony had been able to tune out a little of what Marcus said. But the words *Rae loved me* coming out of Marcus's mouth—Anthony probably would have heard that loud and clear if he'd been in Alaska or someplace. If he'd been at the bottom of the ocean.

Marcus replaced the weight in the rack and sat up. "You have a girlfriend," he said, turning to face Anthony. "Help me figure this out. What am I supposed to do to get Rae back?"

It was like two giants had ahold of him, each one yanking in a different direction. He could almost feel the skin across his chest getting tighter, thinner, starting to rip. The decent thing would be to help Marcus deal with the Rae thing. That's what Anthony *should* want to do. But imagining Rae with Marcus, touching him, kissing him—

"My turn," Anthony said. He gave Marcus a shove with his toe, and Marcus stood up and toweled off the sweaty bench. Anthony stretched out on it. "Take it up twenty pounds," he instructed. He wanted this to hurt. Needed it to.

"You can't be thinking you can press more than me," Marcus protested.

"Just put them on," Anthony answered. He shut his eyes and laid one arm across his chest, using his free hand to push the arm farther, stretching out his muscles. Metal clinked against metal as Marcus adjusted the weights. At least for a few seconds he wasn't running his mouth. Anthony reversed the stretch.

"Ready when you are," Marcus told him.

Anthony opened his eyes, raised his arms over his head, and tightened his fingers around the metal bar. He let out a long, controlled breath as he lifted the weight, then inhaled as he brought it back down. "One."

"So what should I do?" Marcus asked.

Crap. Anthony'd been hoping Marcus would at least let him get through the set before the guy started in again. Anthony lifted the weight again, focusing on his screaming muscles. Was he insane, trying to lift twenty more than Marcus?

"So what did she say, exactly?" Anthony asked, trying to talk and inhale as he brought the weight back down. It was a total girl question. But if he was going to step up and help Marcus, it's what he needed to know.

"She said she couldn't take it because it was too big a thing," Marcus answered. "I think she thought if she took it, it would mean we were getting back together. I told her that taking it didn't have to mean anything. That I wanted her to have it no matter what. But I guess she didn't believe me."

"*I* don't believe you," Anthony said, staring at the weight as he raised it. "You're telling me you shelled out—" He realized he had no idea what a bracelet like that would cost. "All that cash," he finished, breathing hard. "And you weren't expecting Rae to get back together with you because of it?"

"Not right that second," Marcus answered.

"But eventually," Anthony said.

"Yeah," Marcus admitted.

"Obviously she still doesn't trust you," Anthony told him, resting between reps. "You've got to prove you're going to stick around this time." Okay. He'd done it. He'd coughed up some advice, and blood hadn't started running out of his nose or anything.

"So you're saying I just keep being her friend? Just keep hanging around?" Marcus asked.

Anthony gave a grunt, his arms trembling as he heaved the weight back up. "Yeah," he managed to get out.

"For how long?" Marcus said, sounding as whiny as Anthony's littlest brother.

Does it matter? 'Cause if it matters, you don't want it bad enough, Anthony wanted to tell Marcus. "As long as it takes," he forced himself to answer instead.

"What you fear is a huge part of what you are," Ms. Abramson said as she paced around the center of the group therapy circle. "What you fear can determine what you do—or don't do. Who you approach and who you avoid. What you allow yourself to dream about and what forms your nightmares." She gave a sharp clap. "Okay, pair up. I want you to find out as much about your partner's fears as you can."

"Rae, you wanna be—" Jesse Beven began.

Rae was already jerking her metal chair around to face him. She didn't want to talk to anyone about her fears—she didn't even want to think about them. But part of being a good little group therapy participant was vomiting up all your private junk on command. If you didn't, you'd end up in the group until you were a senior citizen. So since she had to spew, she'd rather spew to Jesse. At least he knew her biggest secret already. He knew she was a fingerprint reader; he was the only person besides Anthony and Yana who did.

Jesse and Rae stared at each other. "So I guess I'm going first," Jesse finally said. He started tapping one of his heels against the floor, his leg jerking up and down. "I'm kind of afraid of, uh, dogs. Big dogs, like Dobermans."

Rae nodded, then she noticed Abramson looking at them, standing close enough to hear what they were saying. Rae stifled a sigh. *Just do it,* she told herself. *Put on the show.* "So is there any reason? Did you ever get bitten or anything?" It wasn't exactly a brilliant question, but she was *interacting.* She was *participating.* She was earning her little gold star for the day.

"No. Never even got snapped at or anything." Jesse's leg started bouncing faster. "But I used to have this nightmare where there was this big dog in the hallway outside my room. When I'd wake up, I'd always want—" Jesse hesitated, running his fingers through his red hair as if that would help him figure out the right words. "I'd want to go into my mom's—my parents'—room, to sleep with them, you know. I was really little," he added quickly.

"I used to sleep in my dad's room at least part of every night when I was, I don't know, maybe about three," Rae told him. "Sometimes I'd go in and sleep on the floor by the bottom of the bed. I didn't want to wake him up. I just wanted to be in there."

Jesse shot her a grateful smile, then continued. "I'd get out of bed, and I'd go right up to my door, and I'd crack it open. And then I'd slam it shut real fast. Because even though I knew I was awake and everything, I kept thinking the dog was still out there. Sometimes I could hear it growling. Or, you know, I thought I could. And I was sure it would kill me before I could make it to my mom. The hall was really short, but—" Jesse shrugged.

"So you just stayed in your room by yourself?" Rae asked, her heart cramping for the scared little boy Jesse used to be.

"Yeah. And I kept picturing how big the dog was and how if it really wanted to, maybe it would rip right through my door. Man, I had that dream a couple of times a week for more than a year, I bet," Jesse said. "And dogs, big ones, still give me the creeps."

I wonder if that big scary dog was the dream version of Jesse's dad, Rae thought. Anthony'd told her that Jesse's father had beat up on his mom. And she'd seen for herself how terrified Mrs. Beven was that her ex-husband would somehow track down her and Jesse.

Rae didn't ask Jesse what he thought of her dad/dog theory. Yeah, she wanted to score enough brownie points to make it out of group for good. But there were limits. "Okay, big dogs," she said. "What else?"

"What else?" Jesse repeated. "What else? What else?"

"You're starting to sound like Allison," Rae whispered. Allison was this girl in group who repeated every question Abramson asked her until she thought up some kind of answer. Sometimes Allison would repeat the question seven or eight times.

"What else?" Jesse said again, making his voice a little higher and putting on a heavy southern accent, Allison style. He and Rae both cracked up.

"How's it going over here?" Ms. Abramson dragged a folding chair over to Rae and Jesse and sat down.

"Fine," Rae answered, choking down a laugh.

"Yeah, fine," Jesse said.

"Great. Keep going. I'll just sit in for a while," Ms. Abramson told them. She crossed her arms—her I-lift-weights arms—over her knees and leaned forward, like she was expecting whatever Jesse and Rae had to say to be fascinating.

"I just told Rae that I was afraid of dogs—just big ones," Jesse said. "Now it's her turn."

Rae narrowed her eyes at him. Jesse's turn was in no way over. But Ms. Abramson had already turned her gaze—laser-beam intense—on Rae.

Say something, Rae ordered herself. *Anything.* But it was like someone had mopped out her brain with some of that industrial-strength disinfectant. There was nothing in there. "Um, what am I most afraid of?" Rae muttered, ignoring Jesse's amused snort.

"Not exactly a fun—or easy—thing to think about, I know," Ms. Abramson said, her brown eyes still locked on Rae's face. "Let's try it from a slightly different angle. What are you most afraid to lose?"

"My father," Rae blurted, the answer coming as a blast of emotion. "And An—and my . . . my friends," she added. She cringed inwardly, realizing she'd almost said Anthony—in front of Jesse. Who would of course report every word to Anthony. Jesse treated Anthony like a big brother.

Ms. Abramson leaned even closer to Rae, close enough that Rae could hear each breath Ms. Abramson took. Why was she breathing so fast? She was almost panting. "Anything else?" Ms. Abramson asked.

"Friends and family, that's the big stuff," Rae answered, flashing briefly on Yana. Their fight had left this jagged hole inside Rae, a hole that constantly ached, no matter what Rae was doing or thinking about. *But I'm going to fix things with her,* Rae promised herself.

Rae could feel Ms. Abramson's hot breath against her cheek. "Okay, and how would you be most afraid to die?" Ms. Abramson asked, her voice low and intense.

"What?" Rae exclaimed, giving an involuntary jerk away, the legs of her metal chair squealing.

"Fear of death is probably the biggest fear any of us have," Ms. Abramson explained. "But what is the way that would most terrify you? A long, slow illness? Drowning? Fire?"

My body eating itself the way my mother's did, Rae thought. She couldn't bring herself to speak the fear aloud, although she knew Abramson would love it if Rae had scraped that deep. "Um, drowning would probably be in my top ten," Rae answered. "I don't know how to swim, and being in deep water freaks me out."

I wonder if Anthony and I will ever get back to our swimming lessons, Rae thought, remembering how it had felt to float in the water, his arms holding her up. The lessons had ended after Anthony found out that Rae had tracked down his father for him—and found Tony Fascinelli in prison. But Rae'd always thought they'd get back to them because when Anthony told you he was going to do something, he did it.

"What else would be on your top ten?" Ms. Abramson asked, inching her chair closer to Rae's.

God, does she have to sound so eager? "I—I don't know," Rae muttered. "Probably the same kinds of things anyone would say—fire, dis—" Her voice caught. "Disease, you know," she finished.

Ms. Abramson nodded, and Rae's muscles relaxed slightly. Hopefully all the deep sharing was finally done now.

It didn't seem like Ms. Abramson was ever going to let me out of there, Rae thought as she headed to the parking lot of the Oakvale Institute. Rae'd almost gotten through the group-therapy-room door when Ms. Abramson had pulled her back in and told her that the conversation about fears might bring about some nightmares and that Rae should feel free to call her if she needed to before the next session. Like that would happen. Well, the nightmare part might happen, but Rae didn't plan on calling Ms.

Abramson if it did. These little group therapy sessions were bad enough.

Rae climbed into the passenger seat of her dad's Chevette and closed the door with a soft click. He hated it when people slammed his *baby's* doors.

"How'd it go today?" her father asked as he paper-clipped a page in yet another book about King Arthur.

Rae shrugged. She never knew what to say when her dad asked her about group. "It was fine," she told him when he didn't make a move to put the key in the ignition. "Ms. Abramson, she really focuses on us, you know. She's always telling me I can call her between sessions if I want." Which to Rae seemed at least borderline obsessive, but she figured it would make her dad happy.

"Good for her," Rae's father said. He started the car and pulled out of the parking place. When he got to the driveway, Rae put her hand on his arm.

"Wait. Go right," she burst out. "I want you to drop me off at Anthony's—if it's okay. He'll drive me home from there."

"I live to serve—and chauffeur," her father answered, making the right.

She hadn't seen Anthony since those two seconds before school yesterday. He hadn't been in the caf at lunch, and she didn't have any classes with him.

If she didn't see him soon, she'd go nuts. She needed to look at him at least—maybe that would give her some clue what he was thinking, how he was feeling. Unless he'd already forgotten about kissing her. Unless to him it was no big deal. Was that possible?

Well, let's see, he didn't call you back last night. But that could be because his little brother didn't give him the message. Yeah, she couldn't help adding, *or it could be because he wasn't in the mood. Because unlike you, he doesn't feel like he's going to jump out of his skin if the two of you don't at least talk soon.*

"I've been meaning to ask you, any birthday wishes?" her father said, pulling her away from her thoughts. "Do you want a party? It's getting late, but we could still pull it together for the weekend."

A birthday party. With all my little friends from school. He's probably picturing cake, candles, and pin-the-petal-on-the-daisy. Rae couldn't help smiling as she remembered her father laboriously cutting huge flower petals out of construction paper for her sixth birthday.

"Or we could go out. How about Nacoochee with Anthony and Yana?" her father suggested. "You love that place. Roasted corn chowder. Butterscotch brownie sundaes."

"Maybe," Rae answered. *If Anthony ever voluntarily makes an effort to see me,* she added silently. *If I can convince Yana that I didn't stab her in the back by then.* She'd left Yana at least six messages on her machine yesterday, and nothing.

"Let me know. Whatever you want," her father said. "It's not every day you turn sixteen."

And maybe you won't, a little voice in Rae's head whispered. *You might have what your mom had. And even though it's going slower and you only get the numb spots after you go fingertip-to-fingertip with someone, any day your body could turn on itself.* Rae shook her head, trying to hurl the thought away. That thought—that fear of dying by the wasting disease her mother had—sliced into her brain about a million times a day. She'd be doing something normal, like brushing her teeth, and wham, she'd suddenly picture herself with her teeth falling out, her tongue rotting away. Maybe last time the funny feeling on her tongue had turned out to just be strep throat, but she never stopped imagining what she would do if it came back, and it wasn't strep throat, or anything that could be cured with a simple dose of antibiotics.

"You need to make a left at the light," Rae told her dad. She concentrated on reading every street sign they passed, needing to occupy her brain with something nice and normal. Almost too soon, they turned onto Anthony's street.

"It's the fourth one on the left," Rae said. The last two words came out in a hoarse whisper because all the saliva had evaporated from Rae's throat. Parked in Anthony's driveway was Yana's bright yellow VW Bug.

What's Yana even doing here? Rae wondered, confused. *She and Anthony only know each other because they're both friends with me.*

Or *used* to be friends with her. *Maybe that's why Yana's here,* Rae thought hopefully. She knew Yana had a lot of pride, and it wouldn't be easy for her to say she was sorry for jumping all over Rae the way she had. So maybe she'd come to Anthony instead for advice on how to make up with Rae.

Rae hesitated, trying to process the situation. *Even if that's true, should I really try to talk to either of them right now? It's not like either conversation is something that would work well with an audience.*

Rae's father pulled over to the curb in front of Anthony's house. "You want me to wait and make sure Anthony can bring you home?" he asked.

Rae blinked. Right, her dad. It wasn't like she could suddenly change her mind and tell him to turn around and take her home. He'd worry. And Rae's dad worrying was never a good thing.

"I'm sure he won't mind driving me," she said. She knew Anthony that well. If she didn't have a ride, he'd give her one, whether he liked it or not.

"See you later," she told her dad, then climbed out of the car.

Okay, I can do this, she thought. *I know what I want to say to Yana . . . and to Anthony. Now I just have to say it.* She pulled in a deep breath and started across the front lawn. Through the front window she saw Anthony and Yana sitting together on the couch, Anthony's little sister between them.

She drew in a quick breath—surprised at the sight. It looked like they were just . . . hanging out. Almost like she'd be *intruding* or something. Maybe she should turn around now and go get a bus, or—

Too late. Anthony had spotted her. He was on his feet and heading for the front door.

And life or fate or whatever makes the decision for me, Rae thought. She straightened her shoulders and strode to the front door, reaching it just as Anthony swung it open. "Uh, hi," she said. Those were the only words she could remember. If *uh* even counted as a word.

"Hi," Anthony answered, not making a move to let her into the house.

"What is she doing here?" Rae heard Yana demand.

So, there went the theory about Yana being ready to make up. Rae couldn't believe the tone of Yana's voice—she had no right to sound so mad that Rae was at Anthony's.

"Are you going to make me stand out here on the porch all day?" Rae asked.

Wordlessly Anthony stepped back, allowing Rae inside. The first thing she saw when she entered the hallway was Yana glaring at her, blue eyes bright with anger.

"Yana, uh, hi," Rae managed to get out. "I'm . . . I'm glad you're here. I've been trying to talk to you. Did you get my messa—"

"I am not even going to be in the same room with you," Yana spat out. She turned on her heel and stalked down the hallway and disappeared into the kitchen.

Rae's blood turned to lava. She was surprised her skin wasn't smoking. Yana was supposed to be her best friend, and she wouldn't even give Rae two minutes to—

"She's really pissed off at you," Anthony mumbled.

"Yeah? Well, I'm really pissed off at her," Rae exclaimed. "She should know me too well to think that I'd go behind her back and—forget it. I should be telling her this, not you." Rae took one step down the hall, then Anthony grabbed her by the elbow.

That one touch brought it back again, brought back that moment when her whole world was his hands on her, his mouth on hers.

"I'll talk to her for you," Anthony said, pulling Rae around to face him. "It'll be better. It'll be better if you leave and I—"

"You want me to leave?" Rae asked, a buzzing starting up in her head.

Anthony released her elbow. "Yeah. You should leave."

Chapter 4

I'm the only person on this bus who's alone, Rae realized. *Well, except the driver. And how stupid is it that I'm alone when I'm on my way to the Wilton Center, where very possibly one or more people want me dead? One hundred percent stupid? Criminally stupid? You-should-live-in-a-rubber-room stupid?*

Probably all three. But when Rae'd found the bus stop closest to Anthony's and studied the little maps, she'd found a bus that would take her a block away from the center. The bus had shown up a few minutes later, and Rae had climbed on. It had just seemed like the right thing to do. Although now that the Wilton Center stop was the next one, Rae didn't feel quite so sure she wasn't being . . . stupid. Lethally stupid.

The bus wheezed to a stop, and Rae dutifully climbed off, leaving all the not-alone people behind. *Some kind of plan would be useful here,* she thought.

The block to the center was way too short. For a really brilliant plan you needed a couple of miles at least. For even the most basic plan you needed, well, more than a block. Clearly. Rae hesitated at the edge of the parking lot. *Maybe there's a back way in,* she thought. *If I could manage to get to Aiden's office, I could do a fingerprint sweep and—*

A tall woman hurried out of the main doors of the center. Rae turned around and walked back toward the bus stop. Probably the woman was just someone who took a class at the center. But Rae didn't want anybody to see her near the place. She kept walking until the woman drove past her and disappeared from sight. Disappeared from sight in her *car,* Rae noted, feeling a cartoon-worthy light-bulb go off in her head.

All righty, then, Rae thought. *I've achieved a plan.* She turned around and returned to the center parking lot, reached into her purse, pulled out a tissue, and wiped the wax off her fingertips. It always felt weird when she did that. Like she was getting naked.

Okay, now which of these puppies is Aiden's? she wondered, scanning the cars in the lot. *Probably*

people who work here park close to the front. Rae
made her way to the front of the lot, keeping to the
edge farthest from the main doors. The first car in
the first row was—actually, Rae didn't know what it
was. But it didn't matter what, it mattered who—
who owned the car. Rae lightly ran her fingers over
the driver's-side door handle, getting some static
and—

*I/ have eleven points left/what did Suzi mean/points for wine/any
points/pizza points/*

Somehow I doubt this is Aiden's car, Rae thought,
her stomach gurgling, even though she wasn't hun-
gry. He didn't seem like a guy who'd be on the
Weight Watchers point system.

She moved on to the next car, one of those station wagons with the fake wood.

**/baby blanket/Badger needs food/split nail/shower
gift/**

Too girlie for Aiden, she decided, fighting off the
twinges of not-her jealousy that came with the
shower gift thought.

Rae took a quick scan of the center's windows to
make sure no one was watching her amazing psychic
girl show, then, keeping low, hurried over to the Jeep
parked next to the wagon and slid her fingertips over
the door handle, ignoring the static that she always
got when there were old prints under newer ones.

/record ATM withdrawal/mailing list/half a tank/Jenny/

Okay, wait, wait, wait, Rae thought. She ran her fingers over the door handle again, this time ignoring the thoughts on top and focusing on the static. There were thoughts in there, and she'd caught the words *two girls* in one of them. But that was it.

Rae tried again. All she got were the same two fuzzy words. But the feeling that came with them was much clearer. It was fear, and it made sweat pop out under Rae's arms.

The two girls could be me and Yana. The thought could have come from the day we came to the center and Aiden caught us in the stairwell, Rae thought. She knew she was making a big leap, that *two girls* and the feeling of fear could have come from other situations. But maybe . . .

If you're going to do it, do it fast, Rae told herself. She tried the door. Unlocked. Quickly, trying to look casual, she climbed inside. *Confirmation. I need confirmation,* she told herself. She popped open the glove compartment—

/I need/

—and scrounged around, letting the unfamiliar thoughts zip through her until she found the registration. And the name on it was . . . Aiden Matthews.

So I know it's his car—now what? Rae thought. She couldn't follow him, not without a car of her own.

No, that wasn't quite true. She could follow him from the backseat. It was risky getting in a strange man's car and letting him drive off who knew where. Risky was probably an understatement there. But still, it wasn't as risky as wandering around not knowing who was after her, not knowing if her own body was going to destroy itself. And something in her gut was telling her that Aiden wasn't responsible for her kidnapping. Because she hadn't picked up anything about kidnapping, and she would have if he'd been the second man at the Motel 6. Probably she would have.

I'm not going to be some lost little Rae lamb, she decided as she scrambled into the backseat. She curled up on the floor of the car and covered herself— well, as much of herself as she could—with a jacket she'd found on the seat.

Now all she had to do was wait. When they were far enough away from the center, Rae'd make Aiden pull over and talk to her. She gave a soft snort. Yeah, Rae Voight, nonathlete of the year, was going to *make* a full-grown man do something. Right.

But Aiden probably isn't dangerous, she thought. Probably. Rae closed her eyes and tried not to think. Thinking wouldn't help. There was nothing to plan. It all depended on Aiden and how he reacted when he found out she was there.

* * *

"What's that look?" Yana asked Anthony, sounding annoyed.

Anthony shrugged. "It's my basic watching-TV look," he told her, even though he suspected what had really been on his face was his basic thinking-about-Rae look.

"You were thinking about her, weren't you?" Yana demanded, nailing him. "Getting all worried about her."

Crap. Should he lie? Admit it? Tell her it was none of her business?

"Can we turn the channel to Pokémon?" Anna asked.

Saved by the little sister, Anthony thought. Hanging out with Yana was fun, except when she got on one of her Rae rants.

"No," Danny answered, even though Anna'd been talking to Anthony.

Take Danny to get a haircut, Anthony reminded himself. With all those blond curls getting so long, he was starting to look like a girl, not something that made middle school life very pleasant for a guy.

"You don't get to decide," Anna told Danny. "Anthony gets to decide. He's the oldest."

"Pokémon, Pokémon, Pokémon," Carl, the three-year-old, started to chant. He was about thirty seconds away from a tantrum.

"Sorry," Anthony muttered to Yana.

"It's okay," she answered. Her blue eyes weren't narrowed in anger anymore, and her mouth was soft again, not pressed into a hard line.

"Anthony, Carl and I can watch Pokémon, right?" Anna asked. "Because that's two of us."

"Pokémon," Carl wailed, his face getting red. He was going to blow any second.

"Zack doesn't want to watch Pokémon," Danny told Anna, giving her a little pinch that Anthony knew he wasn't supposed to have seen.

"Zack isn't even in here anymore," Anna shot back. "He's on the phone with his *girlfriend*."

Zack has a girlfriend? Oh, man, Anthony thought.

Carl pulled in a deep breath, and Anthony knew he was about to let out the supersonic scream.

"How about if we play a game?" Yana asked.

Anthony looked over at her, surprised. So did Danny, Anna, and Carl, who had downgraded to defcon 2.

"What kind of game?" Anna asked, squeezing onto the couch next to Yana.

"Ever hear of sardines?" Yana asked, shooting a playful smile at Anthony.

Anna wrinkled her nose. "Like the greasy little fish?"

"That's where the name comes from," Yana answered,

giving Anna's wrinkled nose a light tap. "The game's like hide-and-seek, except in sardines, only one person hides and everyone else looks for them."

The kids like her, Anthony realized. Who would have thought Yana'd be a kid person? *Maybe she wishes she had brothers and sisters,* Anthony thought. *Living alone with her dad and the bimbette of the hour doesn't sound like any picnic.*

"Then when you find the person who's hiding, you get in the hiding place with them," Yana continued. "At the end of the game, one person is looking for everyone else. And everyone else is crammed into one place like . . ." Yana paused, looking from Anna to Danny.

"Sardines," Anna said happily.

"Sardines," Danny muttered, not managing to completely disguise his interest.

"I'll hide first," Yana said. "You guys all close your eyes and count to fifty." Anna, Danny, and Carl all obeyed. "You, too, Anthony," Yana told him. Then she leaned close and whispered, "I'll be waiting for you in the bathroom."

I'll be waiting for you in the bathroom. Somehow, when Yana said those words like that, they sounded way more interesting than they normally would.

Yana reached out and gently smoothed her hand over his eyes, encouraging him to close them. He joined in the counting with his brothers and sisters, thinking about Yana in the bathtub, covered by bubbles. Not that that's what he was going to find when he got to her, but still.

As soon as they reached fifty, Anna and Danny took off in different directions, Carl trotting after Danny. When Anthony was sure the coast was clear, he headed down the hall to the bathroom. He pulled back the tropical-fish-patterned shower curtain and saw Yana sitting on the edge of the tub.

"Hey, Anthony," Anna called from what sounded like the kitchen. "Jesse's on the phone for you."

Yana scooted over to make room for Anthony between her and the wall. "You can call him back," she whispered. "We don't want to ruin the game." She grinned. "The kids are really into it."

"Yeah. Uh-huh. The kids," Anthony answered as he plopped his butt down on the edge of the tub, squeezing into the tiny space she'd left for him. His leg was pressed up against hers, and he could barely move without touching her.

Which seemed fine with her. Almost immediately she laced her hands through his hair and pulled his mouth toward hers. The sink faucet was dripping cold water, but he tuned out the sound, focusing entirely on kissing Yana.

Except that a tiny part of Anthony's brain was

thinking about Rae. And as he deepened the kiss, the thoughts of Rae increased, taking up more of his brain.

Crap. What was wrong with him? Rae was supposed to be with Marcus. He knew that. And Yana was totally hot. And into him. So what in the hell was wrong with him? Now he had a freakin' picture of Rae in his head, her face all hurt because Yana wouldn't talk to her.

"Yan," Anthony murmured against her lips.

"Hmmm," she murmured back.

"I don't think Rae meant to mess up like that with your dad. Writing that letter, that was just her trying to make things better for you."

Yana's body stiffened. "Do you really want to be talking about Rae right now?" she whispered, her breath tickling his face. She didn't wait for him to answer. She just started kissing him again.

Rae was on a conveyor belt, being moved toward . . . she couldn't see what. Dark. And dangerous. She knew whatever was in the darkness was something to be afraid of. She didn't know how she knew, but she did. The conveyor belt gave a jerk, and Rae's eyes snapped open.

She'd dozed off. God, she'd actually dozed off waiting for Aiden to return to his car. And now the car was moving. She'd slept through him getting in, starting the car, and driving off. Rae slowly brought her wrist up in front of her face and peered at her watch. 7:14. She'd been in the car for more than two hours. How much of that had been driving time? Had she fallen asleep almost right away? Where was she?

Okay, okay, calm down, she ordered herself. Her breath was coming out in panicked wheezes, and it was almost impossible to believe Aiden hadn't heard them. *Okay, this is the plan,* she thought. *You'll count to a thousand, then you'll tell Aiden you're here, in a quiet won't-cause-him-to-have-an-accident way.* Rae's breath steadied as she began to count in her head. When she reached a thousand, she kept going, just to be sure that they were far enough away from the Wilton Center. At least that's what she told herself.

A thousand and four. A thousand and five. A thousand and six. *Stop now,* Rae told herself. *You're never going to get to a number where you feel safe, so just do it. Do it now.*

Rae slowly sat up, her body cramping in a dozen different spots after holding still in a small place for so long. "Aiden," she said softly. "I need to—"

His eyes, wide with shock, met hers in the rearview mirror. The car veered to the left, dangerously close to the cars parked along the curb. "Don't move. Don't say anything," Aiden barked. Rae could see the muscles in his neck tense as he carefully and deliberately drove the half block to the nearest strip mall, pulled in, parked, and turned off the car.

Slowly he turned toward her. "Rae Voight," he said, sounding like he was talking to himself. His gaze sharpened on her face, and Rae felt her veins constrict, slowing down the blood flowing through her body. He was just an ordinary-looking forty-something guy, even sort of dorky with his old-guy little ponytail. But there was a coldness in his eyes that she could feel in every drop of her blood. "What exactly are you doing in my car?"

Rae pushed herself up onto the backseat. She wasn't going to have his conversation from the floor. "What exactly am I doing in your car?" she repeated, using Allison's group-therapy technique to give her time to, well, basically, get her brain—her cold brain—working again. "I'll tell you exactly what I'm doing here," Rae said. "I . . . I . . . A woman called my house and told me to meet you at the Motel 6 last Saturday. When I got there, I was tied up and gagged. I might not have lived through it if—"

"And you got into my car? What in the hell were you thinking?" Aiden demanded, sounding a lot like Anthony did when he got pissed off. "Who was it that grabbed you?" He twisted farther around, grabbing the top of the front seat with both hands. "What did they look like? I need to know everything you can remember."

"They had masks on," Rae told him. She could describe one of them, the fake meter reader, because she'd seen him at her house. But she didn't know how much she wanted to let Aiden know *she* knew.

"How many were there?" Aiden's eyes were practically shooting ice pellets.

"Two," Rae answered. Her fingers itched to sweep the top of the front seat, but Aiden still had a death grip on it.

"And what did they say to you? They must have asked you questions. I need to know everything."

You already said that once, Rae thought. *And that tells me that you know a lot. If you didn't, you'd be driving me to the police station right now so I could make a report. Or at least you'd be taking me home.*

"Start with anything," Aiden urged. "A smell. A sound. One detail can help you remember the rest."

"It's not like I'm going to forget anytime soon," Rae answered. She flashed on the feel of the quilted bedspread in the motel, the feel of the blindfold, and the little beads of sweat its warmth had brought out on the skin around her eyes.

"I'm sorry," Aiden said quietly. He released his

hold on the front seat and rubbed his temples. "I'm sorry. It must have been . . . I can hardly imagine how you must have felt. But if you tell me what you remember, there might be some way I can help."

A way he can help. Not the police. Not the FBI. Him. Rae felt like dozens of needles were pricking her from the inside. Who was Aiden Matthews, really? Because he definitely didn't teach pottery or whatever at the community center. She knew from going fingertip-to-fingertip with him the last time that he'd seen her mother at the center and that he had at least some information about experiments done there, possibly on Rae's mother and the other women in her group. But maybe his involvement went a lot deeper. Did he help on the experiments? Run them? Was he trying to find out what she knew so he could protect her kidnappers?

Whatever his deal is, it's safe to tell him what you remember from the motel, Rae thought. If he was connected to the kidnappers, he'd know all that, anyway. But she was suddenly very glad she hadn't admitted that she knew exactly what one of the kidnappers looked like without his mask.

"There's a Winchell's Donuts over there," Aiden said. "We could go in, get a coffee or a soda for you if that would help."

She shook her head. This was the place Rae

needed to be. "I'm okay. I'd rather just get it over with," she answered. Then, trying to make the move look completely natural, Rae rested her hands on the top of the front seat.

I almost killed again/not even a year since/got to take him down/where/Amanda Reese/

Rae's body turned to steel, hard, unbreakable. And cold, so, so cold. It was as if she'd become a machine and she wouldn't be able to make a move until someone picked up a remote control and punched in her orders.

"Are you sure?" she heard Aiden ask, his voice coming in distorted through her cold metal ears. "You look pale."

It's your body. You control it. There's no remote, Rae told herself. She concentrated all her attention on her fingers and managed to make them let go of the front seat. The moment the contact was broken, Rae's body felt like flesh again. Soft flesh. Flesh that could so easily be hurt. What had made Aiden so hard? So—

Rae realized that Aiden was staring at her. She didn't know if he had any idea about the power her mother had. If he did, she didn't want him to suspect Rae had it, too. *Act normal,* she told herself.

"It's just that thinking about being held prisoner, it's like I'm suddenly back there," Rae managed to say. Which was true. But that was minor compared to the oily fear that was crawling through her now. Aiden's thoughts made it very clear that he knew at least one of the men who'd kidnapped her. And that man was a killer—or Aiden thought he was.

"Take your time," Aiden told her. "I know it's hard."

"The men didn't ask me any questions," Rae began. "I thought they would. I thought that's why they'd tricked me into going to the motel," she continued on autopilot. Her head was still full of the thoughts that she'd gotten from Aiden. Did the "killed again" part have to do with Amanda Reese? Had the man Aiden was thinking of killed Mandy's mother? That fit in with Rae's theory. It would explain the killed-her-mother thought on the piece of plastic from the motel.

"And did they—" Aiden hesitated, then plunged on. "Did they draw blood? Or take a tissue sample?"

"No. God, why would you ask that?" Rae burst out. Except she had a decent idea why—maybe there was some way to tell from her blood or cells that she had a power.

"Did they give you anything to eat or drink?" Aiden asked, ignoring Rae's question.

"Tuna sandwich," she answered.

"Did it taste at all unusual?" Aiden pressed.

Translation: Did it taste drugged? Rae thought. "It tasted okay," Rae said. But was it okay? Had she been drugged in the motel? If she had, had they—

"Did you hear any conversation between the two men?" Aiden went on. Suddenly he was like a robot—grilling her with almost no emotion.

"No," Rae said. "Wait, maybe one of them said, 'Get the other one,' or something like that."

"Other one? What did that mean?" Aiden had his hands on top of the seat dividing them again, leaning close.

Is he trying to fake me out? Rae wondered. *Trying to convince me he doesn't know anything at all?* "My friend Yana was at the motel with me," she explained, since she wanted Aiden to think she trusted him. "They kept her there, too."

"And that's all you heard?" Aiden asked.

Rae met his gaze, even though it made her feel cold. "Yeah, that's it."

"Is there anything else you can tell me? It doesn't matter how small." Aiden kept his eyes on hers without blinking.

"No," Rae said. She just wanted to get out of there, get home, home to her own room, home with her dad close by.

"Okay," Aiden replied. "Now listen closely. If I ever need to get in touch with you, I'll say it's because your aunt is sick. Got it? Your aunt is sick. If anyone phones you and claims to be me without using those words, then you call me immediately."

Rae decided to risk one question of her own. "Do you think someone is watching you? Is that how whoever called me knew to use your name? Because whoever it was thought I would trust you enough to meet you."

Aiden took Rae's head in his hands and leaned so close, their faces almost touched. "If you don't do exactly as I say, you could lose everything and everyone you care about." He spoke slowly and deliberately, as if Rae were a very young child. "If you're contacted again, call me. That's all you need to know."

Right, Rae thought. *Just call him. That's easy. That's simple. It's not like every single time I decide who to trust, I'm putting my life in danger.*

Chapter 5

The bell rang. Anthony blinked in surprise. He hadn't been expecting it. And how land of the bizarre was that? Had he ever been in a freakin' class and not known how many minutes until his release? Especially when it was the last class of the day. Most of the time he'd had his eyes on the clock, watching the second hand's final rotation, watching the minute hand click into place.

Anthony grabbed his binder and his reading book and jammed them in his backpack, then headed for the door. "Got a minute?" Jesperson, Anthony's English teacher, asked.

"Uh, sure," Anthony answered, his stomach cramping a little the way it always did when a teacher wanted to talk to him alone. He came to a stop in front of Jesperson's desk. Jesperson was half sitting, half leaning on the edge. The guy hardly ever sat behind it. "What's up?"

"Just wanted to check in with you and see how you're doing. It's a big change moving from Fillmore to here," Jesperson said.

"Big, yeah," Anthony agreed. He knew he should say something else, but he'd gotten a case of Bluebird brain. Nothing but around twenty words in the head anywhere. "But I'm doing okay."

"You like your tutor?" Jesperson asked.

"Yeah, uh-huh," Anthony told him. And it was true. The guy was a book geek, but he never made Anthony feel like a moron. It was kind of like working with Rae. Except the tutor boy didn't smell like citrus and girl. And he didn't trace words on Anthony's skin the way Rae had. Not that Anthony wanted him to. But when Rae did it . . . it was like her fingertip was sexier than other girls' whole bodies.

"And you're making friends?" Jesperson said, sounding like the answer was really important to him.

"The guys on the team," Anthony answered.

"No one else?" Jesperson pressed.

Anthony shrugged. "I've met some people. It hasn't been that long."

Jesperson stood up. "Of course it hasn't. I'm sure in a few more weeks you'll know pretty much everyone around."

"Yeah, uh-huh," Anthony said again. He shifted his weight from one foot to the other. Was that it? Could he go now?

"If you need any help beyond what your tutor can give you—or just want to talk—I'm available." Jesperson clapped Anthony on the back.

"Okay, thanks," Anthony answered, backing toward the door. "See you." He turned and made it through the door, glad to escape before Jesperson said anything else. Anthony'd used most of his twenty words, and besides, there was something about Jesperson. He seemed . . . Anthony shook his head. He seemed a little too interested. Interested wasn't quite it, but something like that.

Whatever, Anthony thought as he hurried down the hall. He made a right, then stopped, his sneakers squeaking. Rae was standing by his locker. Crap. He wasn't up for talking to Rae, not when Yana was probably already in the parking lot, waiting for him. He took a step backward. The locker stop wasn't absolutely necessary. He'd—

He'd go up and talk to her. Because she'd already seen him, was already smiling at him. "Hey," he said as he approached her, her blue eyes pulling on him like a tractor beam. *You'll just make it really fast,* he coached himself. *You'll do the locker book exchange, then say you have football practice and that'll be it.*

Anthony reached for his lock and started dialing in the combination.

"Um, hey," Rae replied. "I was hoping we could maybe go somewhere, like to Chick Filet or something, because you—"

"I can't," Anthony burst out. "I have football—"

"Because you don't have football practice today," Rae continued, speaking over him.

"Right, I know," he said. He'd screwed up his combination, and he started over, trying to look completely focused on it while he frantically tried to come up with a reason why he'd just lied so stupidly. He'd gotten Bluebird brain again. And her grapefruit smell wasn't helping. Nothing was coming to him. All he could think was what if Yana got bored in the parking lot and came into the school, looking for him. He wasn't ready for another Rae-and-Yana scene. Definitely not ready for Rae to see that he and Yana were . . . whatever they were. Even though she should know. Probably.

"I have football the rest of the week is what I was going to say," Anthony finally said. He opened his locker and half buried his head inside it. "Which is why today I'm taking Anna to the dentist," he burst out. "It's the only time I can drive her." He yanked a couple of books out of his backpack, jammed them in his locker, and slammed the door. "She was riding her bike, and she decided to try and do a front wheelie," he explained, still not meeting Rae's gaze. "You know, where you go up on the front wheel. Actually, she didn't decide. Danny talked her into it. He's always talking her into stupid crap. And she chipped a tooth. And so I have to take her to the dentist."

Probably too much information, Anthony thought. But once he'd started telling that story—which had actually happened, but a few years ago—he couldn't stop.

"Ouch. Did it hurt a lot?" Rae asked.

Anthony glanced over at her and felt a little dizzy, like the floor had started slowly spinning under his feet. "What?"

"When she chipped her tooth. Did it hurt?" Listening to her voice was like biting into a lemon. *She doesn't believe me,* Anthony thought. *Best-case scenario, she's not sure whether to believe me or not.*

"It, uh, bled a lot," Anthony said, cursing himself for that *uh* because it would make him sound even more like the liar that he was. *Okay, just get out of here. The more you say, the more chance you're going to screw this up even more.* Anthony clicked the lock back into place. "So, I gotta go. I'll . . . I'll see you."

He bolted. He knew Rae was staring after him, absofreakinlutely knew it. But he didn't turn around.

"So, God, does he think I want to get *married* or what?" Rae typed to the other girls in the Guys Suck chat room. "It was 1 kiss. 1 kiss, and he's lying to my face, coming up with excuses so he won't have to talk to me."

Rae usually didn't bother with chat rooms. The few times she'd peeked in them, they were just full of people handing each other imaginary beers and asking a/s/l, which she'd finally figured out was age, sex, and location. But she'd really needed to vent about Anthony and get some kind of feedback, and since she had no friends—thanks, Yana—she'd been desperate enough to go looking for a chat. And the girls in the room were definitely talking about more interesting stuff than Rae expected.

A bunch of sad little bunnies appeared on the screen, followed by a round red face. The face's cheeks puffed up, its eyes rolled, and then it spewed green puke. *They understand,* Rae thought. Who needed better friends than these? Who needed friends you could actually . . . see, and, like, go shopping with?

"Need more data. Circumstances of kiss, please," dreamgirl said—well, typed.

"There was a fire," Rae typed back. "He carried me out. Then he kissed me." It sounded so dry reduced to those three little sentences. "The most amazing kiss I've ever had," she added. She wished she knew how to make those little animated pictures. She'd show the bunnies swooning. She'd show the face smiling so big that the head cracked in two.

"Movie moment. Wow," dreamgirl replied.

"Does anyone have a tissue?" grrlygrrl typed.

":handing gg a tissue:" Elsinor responded.

Rae's eyes were stinging the tiniest bit, but she didn't ask for a tissue. It would make her feel too goofy. And too pathetic.

"Hate to say it. But life-or-death sitch. Boy can't be held responsible," juliaagogo jumped in.

The puking face reappeared.

"Don't vomit at me," juliaagogo typed. "True. You do stuff in a crisis that you wouldn't usually do."

The puking face—Rae realized it kept coming from someone called ruTHie—appeared again.

"No excuse for lying," Elsinor answered.

"He could be embarrassed," juliaagogo suggested.

Yeah, Rae thought. *Maybe he didn't really mean to do it. Maybe he was just so relieved to get me out of the Motel 6 that he . . . that he . . . that he kissed me.* God, there should be a different word than *kiss* for what Anthony had done. Like melted. *He melted me. He detonated me. He souled me.* Something that sounded much more significant, much more world re-forming than *kiss.*

"That means what he felt was totally different from what I felt," Rae typed in. "'Cause if he felt what I did, he'd—" Rae backspaced over the last line without sending it.

"It happens," grrlygrrl replied. "Happened to me."

"So what do I do?" Rae asked. "How do I get things back to seminormal between us?" Because if Anthony kept hiding out and bolting to keep away from her, she wouldn't be able to take it. She hadn't known Anthony for long, but he'd been there for pretty much all the big events of her life. He'd helped her figure out her power. He was the first person she'd told that her mother was a murderer. He'd saved her *life.*

"Back off," dreamgirl suggested.

"Sucks, but probably right," Elsinor agreed.

A new name appeared in the list of chatters—TabbyTee. "All the same losers, I see," TabbyTee observed. "Don't any of you have anything better to do than whine about guys?"

Rae felt like TabbyTee had thrown a glass of cold water in her face. She did have better things to do.

Vital things. Yeah, Anthony was important to her. Yeah, she wanted to get things back to the way they were if that's all she could have. But what she really needed to do was find a way to make sure she stayed alive. Right this second she should be digging into the death of Amanda Reese.

ruTHie shot out a face that spit fireballs. Elsinor told TabbyTee she wasn't welcome there. Rae typed in another message: "Thx, everybody. Gotta go." She left the room without waiting for replies.

Now what? Rae lightly drummed her fingers over her keyboard, then clicked on the link that would take her from AOL to the Web and found the *Atlanta Journal-Constitution* site. She did a search for Amanda Reese and carjacking. The engine found a match in the Metro section's Law & Order column, where there was a roundup of local crimes, and it slowly loaded. When it was done, she printed it out.

"So short," Rae whispered when she pulled the warm sheet of paper out of her printer. There was just a paragraph for the event that changed Mandy Reese's whole life. Mandy's and her sister's and her dad's. And there were so many other people affected—friends, people Amanda Reese worked with, relatives. But all the paper gave the story was one little paragraph stuck in among the other paragraphs about DWIs and bank robberies and descriptions of people the FBI was looking for.

Carefully Rae began to read. The paragraph didn't tell her much. Date and time of the carjacking. The name of the street where the murder happened. What kind of gun was used. The fact that there had been no witnesses. The fact that there had been a rash of carjackings in the neighborhood. The names of the family members left behind.

It's a newspaper, Rae reminded herself. *Facts are all it's supposed to give.* But it still felt wrong somehow. Couldn't there have been something personal about Amanda? Like what her favorite thing in the world was? Or what place she loved the best? Something that would—

Rae was pulled away from her thoughts by a light tapping on her door. "Come in," she called.

"I wanted to check back with you about your birthday," her father said as he stepped inside.

Rae leaned her head back on the cool black leather of her desk chair. "I haven't thought too much about it yet," she admitted. She saw a flash of concern in his eyes and knew that if she went fingertip-to-fingertip with him right this second, she'd find worries about her, worries about whether her lack of interest in her birthday indicated a deeper problem, a return to the place she'd been in before her breakdown.

"But you know what, Nacoochee is sounding really good. Last night I think I dreamed about their butterscotch brownie sundaes," Rae told him.

"I'll go make reservations," he answered. He took a step back toward the door, then hesitated, rubbing the bump on his nose. "Two or . . ."

"Let's go for two. It'll be fun. Just us," Rae answered. There was no way she was going to ask Anthony. Because Anthony, being Anthony, would go and be all weird the whole time. And Yana. Forget her. She wasn't crawling after Yana anymore. If Yana wanted to be her friend again, then Yana could come to Rae.

"Two. You've got it." Her dad left her room, quietly closing the door behind him.

Rae let out a sigh. Back before The Incident, she'd thought her sixteenth birthday would be this incredible night. She'd spent hours thinking about the place and the guest list and the colors she wanted to use. But now . . . Her birthday felt like something to get through, an occasion where she had to be sure she seemed happy enough so her father wouldn't get all knotted.

She turned her attention back to the computer screen and hit the back button. She scanned the list of articles that were a partial match to her search. One was an obituary for Amanda Reese. Rae didn't bother to read it. She didn't want to see Mandy's mother's life reduced to an even smaller paragraph.

Five of the articles were about carjackings that happened in the two months before Mandy's mom was jacked. Rae printed them out. They were all short. But there was one thing in all of them that got Rae's attention. None of the other drivers had been killed. One man had been knocked out with the butt of a gun, and guns had been used to scare the other drivers out of their cars. But no one else had been shot. And no one else ended up dead.

Rae thought she had an idea why. She suspected that the fake meter reader—if she was right about him being Amanda Reese's killer—had known about the cluster of carjackings and had used them as a cover. He'd probably hoped the police would lump all the jackings together. And from what she'd read, they had.

So I have a piece of the puzzle. But the puzzle is very big. I have no idea what the picture will turn out to be.

More pieces. More information. That's what she needed. And she needed it fast. Because she could feel danger closing in. A killer. And very possibly something within her own body.

Rae flipped back to the list of articles, skimming

each one that could have the slightest connection to Amanda Reese's murder. But she got nothing. Not even a piece of a piece.

What now? she thought. No answer came to her.

"Rae, hey, there."

See, this is what happens when you get so caught up in your thoughts that you stop seeing what's in front of you, Rae thought. "Hi, Mr. Jesperson," she said as she started up the stairs to the school. *Maybe I can just walk right past him. Maybe the hi was enough.*

"You look kind of upset," he commented when she reached him.

"No. I'm good," Rae answered. Why had she gotten to school early? It was at least fifteen minutes until the bell.

"You sure?" Mr. Jesperson asked, touching her lightly on the elbow. "Remember, you don't have to keep up a good front for me. I went through a tough emotional time in college, like I told you."

"I know. And I appreciate your, um, willingness to take the time to check in with me," Rae told him. "But I'm good. Really good."

"Is it getting easier with friends—the awkwardness fading?" Mr. Jesperson's eyes flicked back and forth across her face, searching, searching.

God, he looks so eager for some dirt. He'd love it if I broke down and cried right here, Rae realized. *Or screamed. Or had convulsions, even. It'd keep him going for weeks.*

Rae shifted her backpack from one shoulder to the other, using the maneuver to move a little bit away from Mr. Jesperson without drawing attention to how uncomfortable he made her. From her new position, she could see Marcus signaling to her. "Oh, look, there's one of my friends now," Rae said. "I better go see what he wants. See you in class, Mr. J."

"Bye," he called after her.

Rae didn't glance back. She walked straight over to Marcus. "What's up?"

Marcus ran his fingers through his pretty-boy blond hair. "Look, I know I should be giving you time," he started. "I know that's the smart thing to do. And I will. I am. But I have something I want to give you. It's in my car. Can you—can we—go out there for a minute? Only a minute."

"This thing you have to give me—is it under ten dollars?" Rae asked, struggling to keep her tone teasing. She really didn't need to go through another heavy-duty scenario with Marcus right now. She already felt like a sponge that had been rung out so many times, it was dry as a rock.

"It's free," Marcus assured her. "Well, almost

free. How much do you think three pages of binder paper and some ink cost?"

Rae laughed, and she didn't even have to force it. "I hope you didn't write me a three-page poem. That four-liner one you did that time was bad enough."

"No, there is no rhyming involved." Marcus crossed his heart like a little boy. An adorable little boy. "Come on. We have about ten minutes before class."

Rae followed him out to the parking lot and over to his car. She wasn't sure it was the smartest thing to do, but it was easier than getting out of it. And she had to admit, she was curious. When Marcus climbed into the Range Rover, she got in beside him.

"Okay, well, here it is. My masterpiece." Marcus reached across her, popped the glove compartment, and pulled out sheets of paper. "For you." He thrust the pages into her hands. Rae wondered what she would have picked up if her fingertips weren't coated with wax.

"So, should I read it now?" she asked. She kind of hoped he'd say no. It would probably be easier if she could read it by herself and then plan out what she wanted to say. Yet she was still curious.

"Are you kidding? If you don't read it now, I'll probably go insane." A moment after the word *insane* came out of his mouth, his face flushed a deep, painful-looking red. "I didn't mean to—"

"It's just some sounds," Rae told him. But her curiosity seeped away. She couldn't help remembering how Marcus had been when she was in the hospital. Or how he hadn't been. He'd barely come to see her. Yet he'd found time to hook up with Dori.

"Read it, okay?" Marcus smoothed out the papers. Rae hadn't realized she'd crumpled them.

"Okay," Rae said. She raised the first page up in front of her so it would hide her expression from Marcus. "Things I—" She pulled in a deep breath. "Things I love about Rae," she finished in a clear voice.

Her eyes ran down the list, picking up random words and phrases. That was all she could take right now. *Cheesecake monster, earlobes, March 9, 11:14, Raemondo, nuggle bunny, the drawing of me, butterfly kiss, mispronounce middle name, cries watching* Frosty the Snowman, *bubble gum lips.*

Rae couldn't turn this page over. And there was no way she could move on to the second page. "Marcus, this is so sweet," she said, her voice trembling with emotion.

Marcus gently took the list away from her. He leaned close, and she knew he wanted to kiss her. She didn't try to stop him. She closed her eyes, waited, and then felt his lips lightly brush against hers.

It felt . . . nice.

Rae opened her eyes and got busy picking up the list and folding it. "This was, is, was, so sweet," she said again.

The kiss was sweet, too. But she felt not even a spark of what she'd felt when Anthony kissed her. She realized that even during their wildest make-out sessions, when Marcus's hands were moving all over her body, she'd never felt the way she did during that one kiss with Anthony.

Not that Anthony gave any sign of ever wanting to kiss her again. But now that she'd realized what a kiss could feel like, how could she return to sweet? There had to be somebody out there who could make her feel the way Anthony did. Someone besides Anthony.

"Rae?" Marcus said. Her name formed a question, *the* question. Did she still love him? Half of her wanted to say yes and throw herself into Marcus's arms. Where it would be safe, safe and sweet.

"Marcus," Rae managed to get out through the lump that had formed in her throat. The way she said his name gave him his answer. She could see it in his face, in his eyes, before he turned away.

Chapter 6

"I don't know what was going on in the first half," Coach Mosier said, speaking so softly, Anthony could barely hear him. "I don't want to know," he continued. "All I want is for it to stop. You have fifteen minutes to figure out how to accomplish that."

He turned around, walked slowly and deliberately to his office, and shut the door behind him with extreme care. A moment later the blinds slithered down, covering the big window that looked out over the locker room.

Anthony hadn't been on the team for long, but long enough to know that Mosier was a yeller. When you did good, he yelled. When you screwed up, he yelled louder.

"Do you think he's really a robot?" McHugh asked. "Or possessed by an alien, like in that movie *The Faculty*?"

"He is *pissed*," Sanders said. "If we don't figure out a way to turn this around—"

"We don't need fifteen minutes for that," Ellison interrupted. "We don't need fifteen seconds. All we need to decide is who's going to take Salkow out back and put him out of his misery."

"Shut up," Marcus muttered, eyes on his feet.

"The man speaks the truth," McHugh bellowed, looping his arm around Ellison's shoulders. "And the truth cannot be silenced."

No one laughed. The thing was, Ellison was right. Marcus had been messing up since the first play of the game. It was like somebody had opened up the guy's brain and fried every part that knew anything about football. They'd removed some muscles from his hands, too. Or that's the way it had looked out there from the number of times Marcus had dropped the ball.

"What *was* going on with you?" Sanders asked Marcus.

"Nothing, all right? You worry about yourself, Sanders," Marcus snapped. "Like none of the rest of you have ever messed up," he muttered as he stalked toward the Gatorade cooler. He grabbed a bottle and chugged it without returning to the group.

"Maybe he's on the rag," McHugh suggested. He got a few guilty-sounding laughs with that one.

Anthony expected one of the guys to go over and talk to Marcus. But no one made a move. *Okay, so I guess it'll be me,* Anthony thought. *And why the hell not? I'm the guy's friggin' Dear Abby.* He grabbed a towel off the closest bench and wiped some of the sweat out of his hair as he made his way over to the cooler. He grabbed an orange-flavored Gatorade and took a swig. Because he had no idea what to say. He had no idea why he'd even thought that he should attempt to say something.

"I know you said I should give Rae time," Marcus burst out.

Crap, Anthony thought. *Rae again. Crap.*

"But I couldn't just wait around, doing nothing," Marcus continued.

Anthony squeezed his eyes shut for a moment. "What did you do?" he asked.

"I made a list of all this stuff about her. A stuff-I-love-about-Rae list," Marcus answered. "A girl should die for something like that, right? I mean, Dori would have—"

"You didn't start going out with another girl while Dori was in the hospital," Anthony cut in. He knew he was supposed to be helping Marcus get back into game head, not busting his chops, but the words had come out flying out of his mouth.

"Yeah, yeah, I know," Marcus mumbled. "But the list. You should have seen it. It was three pages long. And it had everything on it. Like how she used to call me nuggle bunny, which came from snuggle bunny, which she thought up one night when—"

"I get it," Anthony said, cutting him off and taking another long swallow of his Gatorade to wash the bitter taste out of his throat. "So what was the upshot? What'd she say when you gave it to her?"

Marcus shook his head. "She said she wasn't ready to get back together. That's it. But the way she said it, it was, like, I don't know, like she'd already decided it was never going to happen."

Cords of heat shot from his belly up and down his body, like he was having an internal power surge. *What, you think because Rae doesn't want Marcus today that means something?* Anthony asked himself. *Yana told you that she's still in love with him, remember? The girl is obviously just getting a little payback. And good for her.* Marcus deserved to be tortured for a while.

Anthony glanced over to where the other guys were huddled. Time to get back on track. "So, the

Rae thing, is that why you're having trouble . . . concentrating out there?"

"I guess." Marcus dropped back his head and sighed. "It's like I keep thinking there's something I can do to make her change her mind right now."

"I already told you what I thought," Anthony answered. "You've gotta prove yourself to her. And that could take a while." He forced himself to go on. "But it'll happen. I, uh, heard one of her friends saying that she's not over you."

Marcus's head snapped up. "Really? Who said it?"

Anthony felt like he'd eaten an ice cream cone too fast. There was this cold pain building behind his eyes. He ignored it and gave a shrug. "I don't know her name. But the girl sounded like she knew Rae pretty well."

"You're sure you heard her right?" Marcus asked.

"Yeah. So you think you can pull your head out now and get us through the rest of the game?" Anthony asked.

Marcus smiled. A ridiculously big smile. "I think I can manage that. Now that I know I've still got a chance with Rae."

Why'd you even doubt you would get what you want? Anthony wondered. *Don't you know guys like you always do?*

* * *

"So, you think the guy who kidnapped me is the same guy who killed this girl's mother?" Jesse asked Rae as they headed down Mandy Reese's street. "And also the same guy who tried to off you?"

"Yeah. I'm not absolutely sure, but yeah," Rae told him.

Jesse nodded. Rae could see the muscles in his throat working. "What are we going to do when we find him?" he asked.

"Turn him over to the police, I guess," Rae said. She couldn't believe she'd never thought about that. "All I care about is that he's kept far away from all of us."

"Better ways of doing that," Jesse muttered. His eyes seemed to be made of blue steel, and for that instant he looked . . . inhuman.

"Let's worry about finding him for now," Rae said.

Maybe I shouldn't have brought him here, she thought. *I could have figured out a way to distract Mandy on my own.* She shot another look at Jesse. *He really looks like he could . . . God, like he's prepared to kill someone. I should have left him out of this. It's not good for him.*

Too late now, she told herself. And she had to admit it felt good to have someone on her side again. Especially considering what she was about to do. It had seemed so obvious when the thought struck her this morning—the fact that there was another way to learn more about Amanda Reese's murder. Mandy had told her and Yana that the car her mother was carjacked in was back at her house, sitting in the garage and never used anymore. Which meant it probably had some prints on it— possibly prints that could give Rae a clue about Amanda Reese's killer. Still, the prospect of getting up close and personal with the car Amanda had been in before she was . . . Well, it wasn't something Rae was looking forward to.

"Mandy's is that yellow house up there," Rae said, pointing it out to Jesse. She picked up her pace, almost trotting when she swung up Mandy's front walk. "You ready?" she asked him when they reached the door.

Jesse snorted. Rae took that as a yes and rang the bell. Mandy answered so quickly that Rae suspected she'd been standing a foot away, waiting for them. "Thanks for letting me come over again," Rae said. "I was wondering if I could see that group picture with my mom in it again. I don't have that many of her." It wasn't true, but it pretty much guaranteed Mandy's cooperation.

"Sure. Um, who's that?" Mandy jerked her chin toward Jesse.

"Oops. And my dad actually did force me to go to charm school when I was, like, eight. He was worried that I'd miss out on critical mom socializing, I think." Rae gave a polite smile. "Mandy, I'd like you to meet Jesse. Jesse likes skateboarding and comic books. And Jesse, this is Mandy. Mandy, well, honestly, I don't know. Mandy, what do you like?"

"Well, um, I, God, I can't think of anything." Rae noticed that Mandy kept shooting Jesse these little looks. *He is a cutie,* she realized. She'd never thought about how a girl Jesse's age would see him.

"Doesn't matter," Jesse told Mandy. "Rae's being an idiot."

Thank you, Jesse, Rae thought. But she couldn't get even a little irritation going because she could see that Jesse was shooting little looks right back at Mandy. *Wonder when she'll realize she hasn't asked us in.*

"Oh!" Mandy said about three seconds later. She backed up into the door, gave another "oh!" and managed to usher Rae and Jesse into the house. "I'll go get that picture. You guys wait in the living room."

Rae wondered what Jesse would think of Mandy if he could see her bedroom. It was even more of a mess than his. He probably wouldn't care. Unless he thought of girls as a whole separate species and was shocked that one actually lived surrounded by pizza boxes and dirty socks.

"Aren't you going to go?" Jesse whispered to Rae.

"Yeah. Of course. You just tell Mandy I'm in the bathroom and keep her talking until I get back," Rae answered. She headed down the hall, slowing down when she caught sight of the kitchen. She inched inside and took a peek. Empty. Good. She didn't want to deal with Mandy's sister, if she was even home.

Now, there's the door that I'm hoping goes to the garage, Rae thought as she hurried to the door she spotted next to the fridge. She pulled it open. Cool, musty air hit her face, and she shivered. On the other side of the garage she could see what she assumed was *the car,* the car Mandy's mother had been driving the day she died. It was covered in a tarp, and Rae couldn't help thinking it looked like a ghost. She hesitated, not wanting to get close to it. *It's just a car,* she told herself. *Yeah,* a part of her answered. *Just a car where somebody died.*

"She didn't die in the car," Rae whispered to herself as she forced her feet to start moving across the garage. "They pulled her out." When she reached the car, she whipped off the tarp without hesitating. She didn't want to give herself time to get more creeped out.

Now get in, she ordered herself. Her body didn't obey. Instead Rae carefully folded the tarp, making sure all the edges were even. *Okay, now get in,* she ordered herself again. But her body didn't move. *You've got to do this. Mandy's going to be back any—*

That thought got her moving. She gently ran her fingers over the door handle, picking up a burst of static. She couldn't make out a single word. *A lot of people touched this car after the accident,* she thought. *But there's got to be something left.*

Rae opened the door and slid into the driver's seat. *She was sitting here seconds before she died.* The thought flashed through Rae's mind before she could stop it, and everyplace her body touched the seat began to itch, even though her skin was protected by a layer of clothing. Ignoring the sensation, she lightly rested all ten fingertips on the steering wheel. More static. Rae ran her fingers over the ridges of the wheel, not wanting to leave an eighth of an inch untouched. Static. Static. But a different kind, she thought. Like from those white noise machines some people used to block out sounds while they slept.

The police probably dusted the whole thing for prints, Rae thought. *It's distorted the thoughts even more than usual.* She moved her hands from the wheel to the dashboard, then from the dashboard to the sun visors, from the sun visors to the rearview mirror. Just more of the same soft, eerie shushing. *Under that sound, Amanda's trying to tell me something. I know it,* Rae thought.

She traced the front of the glove box, the shushing, hissing white noise sounding like a ghostly voice to her now, a voice begging to be understood. "I want to hear what you have to say," Rae said. The hairs on the back of her neck and her arms stood up because it felt like someone was listening.

Rae jerked her head to the garage door. It was closed, just as she'd left it. She was still alone. But it didn't feel that way.

"Amanda, if you're here, I want to help you," Rae said, her voice sounding way too loud in the enclosed space of the car. *You're letting your imagination get out of control,* she told herself. *Amanda isn't here. Amanda is dead.*

Try the seat belt. The idea came to her as bright and clear as a neon sign. The seat belt would have been dusted, too, but she ran her fingers over the metal insert. *Shhhhh.* She ran her fingers over the plastic buckle and release button. *Shhhhh.* She ran her fingers over the webbed strap.

/ShhhhHlMhhh/

Rae's heart felt like it had been zapped with the

103

paddles of one of those machines doctors used to bring people back to life. Her body actually convulsed. She moved her fingers back and inch.

/ShhhhHIMhhh/

That one thought, that *HIM,* was filled with knowledge. And it had the flavor of the thoughts she'd gotten from Amanda's belongings. *She knew the person who killed her,* Rae realized. Knew him and was terrified by the sight of him. Rae continued running her fingers along the belt but got nothing except the white noise. The ghost voice. She knew it was just a different version of the static, but God, it felt like Amanda was trying to talk to her.

Rae scanned the passenger-side seat belt, the headrests, the entire length of the seat. *Shhhhh.* That was all. But it felt more insistent. *It feels that way because you've scared yourself. That's all,* Rae thought.

She got another neon-sign idea. The floor mat. Rae climbed out of the car and crouched next to it so she could search the floor mat, although she didn't know why Amanda would have gotten any fingerprints on it. The answer came to her as soon as the thought was formed. She was being dragged out of the car, and she grabbed the mat.

Whoa. Where did that come from? Rae wondered. Did it come from Amanda? Could Amanda be guiding her? *Get a grip,* Rae thought. *You know Amanda was pulled from her car, and you made a logical leap. And anyway, you don't even know for sure that there are prints on the mat.*

All her muscles tensed as she reached out one hand and tentatively touched the black rubber.

/ShhhILLshhh/

Rae backtracked with her fingers.

/ShhhKILLhhh/

Another shock to her heart. "Clear," Rae muttered, rubbing her chest with her free hand while tracing the area where she'd gotten the thought.

/kill us all/

An absolutely clear one. Like a voice speaking in Rae's ear. Rae noticed there was a tiny nick in the rubber just outside where her fingers were positioned. *Amanda did that with her fingernail,* she thought. *God, I'm having those logic leaps all over the place.* Suddenly she wanted to get out of the garage. Okay, not suddenly. She'd wanted out of the garage since she stepped into it. But now it was like the air was getting sucked out of the place, like Rae would die if she stayed.

There's plenty of air, she told herself, pulling in a deep breath as proof. She continued searching the mat, the shushing sounds feeling like they were wrapping her in cotton, filling her nose, filling her mouth. She really couldn't breathe.

Yes, you can, she thought, taking a long, slow breath while her fingers continued to move.

/shhhWARNhhh/THEhhhh/GROUhhh/

Hot tears filled Rae's eyes. She didn't know if they were hers or if they were coming from Amanda's emotions. *She never got to warn the group,* Rae thought. *How many of the others did he kill? Every time I tried to contact someone from the group and got a new resident or a no-new-number message, every time that happened—was the person dead?* Rae's breath started to come in pants. It was too huge. Too horrible. She couldn't take it in.

Got to calm down, she thought. *Got to finish what I came to do.* As quickly as she could, Rae searched the rest of the car, the chilling whisper of the white noise accompanying her. The second she was done, she threw the tarp back over the car, forced herself to take three precious seconds to straighten it, then ran back into the kitchen and shoved the door shut behind her, forgetting that she was supposed to have been in the bathroom and not the garage.

You're okay. You're okay. You're okay. She kept up the reassuring mental chant as she rushed back into the living room. A strange sound greeted her. It took her a moment to realize it was laughter. Jesse and Mandy were laughing. She'd gotten so used to the shushing sound that human laughter sounded bizarre to her.

"Are you okay?" Mandy asked, catching sight of her. "Jesse said you got sick to your stomach."

"I'm fine," Rae answered. *But is Mandy?* she wondered.

Rae was so sure that the person who tried to kill her killed Mandy's mother. Mandy's mother and who knew how many others. And the reason they'd tried to kill Rae was because Rae's mother was in the group. Did that mean Mandy was in danger? Was Mandy being watched, too? Was *he* waiting for the chance to—

Get some facts, Rae told herself. "Did you find the picture?" she asked Mandy.

"Oh, yeah." Mandy bent down to the coffee table and picked up the photo. Rae reached for it, allowing her fingertips to touch Mandy's.

A tidal wave of thoughts and emotions crashed down on Rae, almost knocking her off her feet. There was so much grief. Anger. And there, right there, a little swirl of excitement and pleasure along with Jesse's name. Rae pushed it aside. Was there any fear? Any feeling of being watched? Anything suspicious?

Rae took in as much as she could and found nothing to make her think anyone was after Mandy. At least not yet.

Chapter 7

istill don't know who else is so interested in my Rae. But I do know that whoever it is would also be interested in me—if they knew the truth about me. I need to know exactly who this potential threat is. I can't keep myself safe if I don't know who might be coming after me. And so I must keep her alive. For now. And watch her to discover who might want to watch me.

But that doesn't mean I can't have any fun. I've decided that I will be a cat, and Rae, Rae will be my little mousie. I will bat her with my paw, scrape her with my sharp white teeth. Terrify her. Leave her squeaking and trembling.

Yes, there's a lot of pain that Rae can experience before she dies, so maybe it's better this way. She deserves all the pain I can inflict. Then she deserves to die.

* * *

Country-western music began to play on the clock radio. Extremely high-fat cheese. *Very funny, Dad,* Rae thought. Clearly he'd fiddled with the settings. She grabbed her pillow and pulled it over her head, trying to block out the whiny voice. Rolling over and turning off the radio would work better, but Rae wasn't ready to wake up to that degree yet. Just a few more minutes. That's all she needed.

But she couldn't go back to sleep. It was too late. She'd already remembered the numb spot that had appeared after she'd gone fingerprint-to-fingerprint with Mandy. *It'll probably be a lot better already,* Rae told herself. Tentatively she brought her hand up to her left side and traced one finger along her ribs. She didn't feel it. She pressed a little harder, scraping the skin with her nail. It hurt. Good. By the end of the day the spot would probably be completely back to normal.

Either that or every time she got a numb spot, it would last a little longer, and she'd eventually end up dead. Sleep, even a few more extra minutes, no longer held any appeal. Rae threw the pillow on the floor, rolled onto her side—and felt something hard underneath her cheek.

Weird, she thought. She pulled out the object and held it up in front of her eyes. It was about half the size of her thumb, and it was wrapped in lavender tissue paper.

Maybe it's another lame-o joke from Dad, she thought. But her heart had its doubts. It was pounding like it wanted to escape from her chest.

Rae sat up and tore away the paper. Her fingers cramped, and she dropped the bullet on her comforter. A bullet. She'd been holding a bullet. She forced herself to pick it up again. Wiped clean. No prints. No thoughts. Carefully, as if it could go off even without a gun, Rae placed the bullet on her nightstand. Just as carefully she climbed out of bed. She reached for the tissue paper and realized there was writing on it. The word *Amanda* caught her eye. She stared at the name, repeating it over and over in her mind until it became meaningless, just a jumble of sounds.

You've got to read the rest, she told herself, then she smoothed out the torn tissue paper, scanning for prints, getting none, until the note written on it was revealed:

It happened to Amanda. It could happen to you. Stay away from places you don't belong.

The tissue paper turned damp in her fingers, damp with sweat. Someone had been in her house.

In her room. Staring down at her while she was asleep. She got a flash of the fake meter reader guy leaning close to her, sliding his hand close to her face.

But the doors were locked. The windows were locked. Rae checked them every night before she went to bed. *Yeah,* she told herself. *But you're dealing with a guy who has put bugs in Anthony and Yana's cars. A guy who has been taking pictures of you with a camera that has an extreme telephoto lens. A guy who paid someone to plant a pipe bomb at Oakvale. A guy like that wouldn't have a problem picking a lock or hiring someone who could.*

Rae rolled the note between her sweaty palms until it formed a tiny ball. A little nothing of a thing. But there was still the bullet. She couldn't turn it into a insignificant wet wad. No matter what she did, it would remain hard and lethal.

And my special friend, the one who's always watching me, he has lots more bullets. I could be walking to school tomorrow and bam. I could be in the caf and bam. I could be back in my own bed tomorrow night and bam. No place is safe for me.

Eat in the weight room or eat in the cafeteria? Anthony asked himself as he left English class. The answer was easy. He wanted to eat wherever

Marcus wasn't. Hearing Marcus go on and on about Rae wasn't something that got the appetite going. In fact, it made him want to spew. *So I'll do a fast check of the—*

The sensation of his butt being slapped made Anthony's brain sputter, the thought left uncompleted. He turned around and saw Yana grinning at him, her blue eyes sparkling. "I had to come over and do that," she told him.

"You had to drive here from your school to grab my butt?" Anthony asked, automatically checking the hall for Rae. Not that he was doing anything wrong.

"Well, that, and to take you to my favorite taco place for lunch," Yana explained. "Three of those rolled ones for a buck. My treat."

"I'm there," Anthony said. Yana had started leading the way out of the building before the words were out of his mouth. *She's pretty freakin' confident,* Anthony thought.

And why shouldn't she be? Like he'd say no. It was damn flattering to have a hot girl like Yana go out of her way to be with him. She was always showing up—at practice or even dropping by his house. And he was always glad to see her.

Except . . . except did her showing up all the time mean that she was thinking . . . Anthony didn't know exactly what to be afraid she was thinking. Who knew what went on in a girl's brain? But was she thinking something like that they were a couple? Or that she was falling in love with him? Because that—that would suck.

As he and Yana headed across the parking lot toward her Bug, she looped her arm around his waist and gave his side a light squeeze with her hand. He'd never thought such a small touch could affect him like that, but with Yana . . .

Focus, Anthony told himself. *Focus using your head. If she is thinking that something—what's the girl word? Serious. If she's thinking something serious is happening between us, then you've got to shut her down.* Anthony climbed into Yana's car and slammed the door.

Yana sped out of the lot in her usual hell-on-wheels way. He glanced over at her, trying to figure out how he could find out if she thought they were in the serious zone. *You're gonna have to come out and ask her,* he told himself. *There's no way you can figure it out in the girl way by analyzing her every move.* That's what his mother did. Anthony still remembered her being on the phone for hours with one of her friends, talking about Tom and what it meant when he said this, and what it meant when he did that, and that it had to mean he definitely liked her because he tried not to burp in front of her. Anthony'd never be able to think that way. *So, go ahead, ask her.*

"Um," Anthony said. And that's all he could get to come out of his mouth.

"Um?" Yana repeated, raising an eyebrow.

"Um." Anthony's brain stalled again. It was like being back in Bluebird English class. "I was thinking about us." Did he actually say that? He started tapping the heel of one foot up and down, making his whole leg jerk. How could he have used the word *us* like that? His whole point was that there wasn't an us. "About you and me," he corrected himself. "Do you? You don't—you're not, uh, serious, are you? Serious about. . . ." He didn't want to say another *us,* so he gestured back and forth between them.

Yana laughed. "Get over yourself, Fascinelli. I definitely haven't decided that I can't live without you."

"Good," Anthony blurted. *Didn't have to sound quite so relieved,* he told himself.

Yana swung into the Taquito parking lot and sped around to the end of the drive-through line. "I like hanging with you. That's it. Your basic fun." She pulled up to the speaker and ordered without asking Anthony what he wanted, then turned back around to face him. "So, feel better?" With one finger she traced a line along his leg.

"Better. Yeah," Anthony choked out as Yana began tracing little circles on the inside of his leg, just above his knee.

Someone blasted a car horn behind them, and Yana drove up to the window, paid for their food, then found a parking spot in the corner under the shade of a big tree. The branches brushed against the windshield and front windows, making kind of a cave.

Yana thrust the bag of food at Anthony. It was hot in his hands, but not anywhere near as hot as that spot on his leg Yana had been working on with her finger. Anthony set the bag on the floor. He had no interest in food right now. All he wanted was to feel her hands on him again.

"Oh, Rae's dad called me last night," Yana said.

Anthony felt like he'd spilled his entire Dr. Pepper on his lap, including the crushed ice. But Yana was still holding the bag with the drinks. "Rae's dad?" he repeated, trying to sound like he hadn't just gone from scalding to freezing.

"Yeah. Rae's birthday is this weekend," Yana told him. "Her dad wants you and me to meet them at some restaurant, do the cake-and-candles thing. I told him we would."

"I thought you—" Anthony began.

"—hate and despise Rae?" Yana finished for him. She pulled her milk shake out of the bag and handed Anthony's soda to him. "I *am* still mad about what she did. But she's my friend. And it's her birthday. So what can I do?"

Anthony nodded. "It's hard to be completely mad at Rae even when she does something that stupid," he said.

He tried to picture himself walking into a restaurant with Yana, making it clear to Rae that he and Yana were together. Not serious or anything, but still.

It's what you wanted, he told himself. *It makes sense for you to be with someone like Yana. Someone who's a lot more like you, who gets your life. Just like it makes sense for Rae to be with some Marcus type, if not the actual Marcus.*

It would be good for it all to be out in the open. That way he and Rae and Yana could all hang out together. The way they used to. Sort of the way they used to.

"So do I look okay?" Rae asked Jesse when they climbed off the bus. "I mean, do I look different enough?" She gave her short black wig a tug. She still couldn't quite believe she'd gotten all her curly hair hidden under it.

"You look amazing," Jesse said, talking to her breasts—her padded breasts. Rae laughed, and Jesse must have realized that he'd been caught ogling, because he blushed. The freckles on his red cheeks reminded Rae of the little seeds in raspberry jam.

"Thanks," Rae answered. "I did my makeup in a much more dramatic way then usual," she added, letting him off the hook.

His blush faded a little. "Yeah. I noticed," he said. Rae managed to hold back a giggle. "I bet Anthony would like to see the new you," he added. He paused. "I kinda thought maybe he'd be here," he continued, the hurt in his voice obvious.

All desire to laugh disappeared. "Anthony's pretty busy, with practice and getting up to speed at a new school," Rae answered.

"Yeah, I noticed," Jesse muttered.

Rae bit her lip, figuring Jesse needed a distraction from the Anthony topic as much as she did. "The Wilton Center is only a block away," she told him. "The main thing we're looking for once we get inside is any kind of info on the experiments or—"

"I got it," Jesse interrupted. "We've already talked about this, like, a hundred times."

"You're right," Rae answered. "So let's just go. Remember that I'm your sister and you want to take a woodworking—"

"I. Got. It," Jesse said. "It's this way, right?" Without waiting for Rae to answer, Jesse started down the street.

"Right." Rae fell into step beside him. A moment later the center came into view. Rae grabbed Jesse by the elbow, getting a few fuzzy thoughts off his shirt. "Look, I know I already told you this, too, but listen one more time, okay?" She rushed on. "Even with the disguise, there's a chance that whoever sent me the bullet is watching us right now. In the note I got, they admitted they killed Mandy's mom. More like bragged about it. I don't think whoever it is—the fake meter reader guy, whoever he really is—will have any problem with killing somebody again. I just—"

"You just don't want anything bad to happen to me," Jesse finished for her.

"I don't want you to end up dead," Rae corrected, wanting him to think about exactly what he was getting in to. "I know you—"

"Shut up, okay?" Jesse cut in, reminding her of Anthony for a second. "This isn't all about you. This guy, he kidnapped me. And Mandy, he practically destroyed her life. Plus he tried to kill you," he added quickly.

Less than an hour with Mandy and he's already so protective of her, Rae thought. Her chest began to ache, as if someone was trying to pull her heart in four different directions. It was so sweet, how Jesse'd reacted to Mandy. But it made Rae feel so alone.

Get over it, she ordered herself. *Not the time. If there ever is a time for rampaging self-pity.* She and Jesse cut across the parking lot and strolled through the main entrance. They'd tried to time their arrival so that classes would be in session, and it looked like they'd gotten it right. The halls were empty.

"Any ideas about where to find the security monitors?" Rae asked softly.

Jesse shrugged. "Where'd you go last time?"

"To the right," Rae answered.

"So let's try left," Jesse said.

God, this place is just so *normal,* Rae thought as they started down the hallway, walking past a row of clearly handmade kites in bright, cheerful colors. And that made it worse. Something so dark and twisted should never have happened here, where kids painted their favorite cartoon characters on kites.

"I think that's the security guard's room down there," Jesse said, pulling Rae out of her thoughts. "You hang back. I'll get him out."

"Do you want to go over what you're—" Rae began. Jesse started to run, so all she could do was watch him go. When he reached the door of the security room, he pounded with both fists. A moment later the door was whipped open by a rent-a-cop, who gave off vibes like those navy SEAL guys.

Rae turned toward the display of kites but listened to every word. "What?" the rent-a-cop barked.

"I was in the bathroom, and there was this guy in there and his backpack was partway open and I saw a gun in there," Jesse blurted, his voice high and breathless.

Oh, no. Not the best story, Rae thought. *The rent-a-cop could have watched us come in on one of the monitors. He could know Jesse didn't go into the bathroom. He could—*

"Is he still in the bathroom?" the rent-a-cop demanded. Rae let out a breath she hadn't realized she'd been holding.

"He was when I left. And I ran down here," Jesse answered.

"Show me," the rent-a-cop said.

Rae remained facing the kites until Jesse and the rent-a-cop had pounded past her. She waited another thirty seconds, took a quick glance to make sure they were out of sight, then hurried over to the security room. *Hope the door isn't one of the ones that lock automatically,* she thought. She grabbed the doorknob, turned it, and pulled. There was the tiniest bit of resistance, then the door swung open. Rae smiled when she saw the wad of gum that prevented the door from clicking all the way closed. "An oldie but a goodie, as my dad would say," she murmured as she stepped inside.

Instantly her eyes went to the row of TV monitors and flicked from screen to screen. Front entrance. Storage room. Pottery class. Hallway. Hallway. Flamenco dance class. Stairway. Office. Yoga class. Hallway. Stairway. Her eyes darted faster. *Nothing here,* she realized.

I guess it was a stupid plan. Like Jesse and I could just prance in here, find the security monitors and—whoo-hoo—get all the answers.

Rae did a scan of the room, although it was too small to hide much of anything.

Except another door! Rae hadn't even noticed it at first. She'd been completely focused on the monitor screens, and you actually had to look closely to notice that there was a thin line going all the way around one part of the wall. It had to be a door.

With two steps she was over to it, then she pushed aside some boxes covering up one side. *Yes.* There was a handle. A door handle. She jerked on it. /extra pay/*sickos*/pick up milk/

Locked. Of course it was locked. Maybe she

could try to get it open with a paper clip or something. Although that was probably as delusional as plan A had been. Rae did a fast check of the monitors and spotted Jesse and the rent-a-cop. They were heading into a classroom. Thank God, Jesse was a good talker.

Rae opened her purse and rooted through, ignoring her old thoughts, until she found a hair clip with an end that she thought would be thin enough to try on the lock.

"Just one problem," she muttered when she returned her attention to the door. "There is no lock." Which meant there had to be—yep, there was one of those little keypads to one side. Rae ran her fingers over the buttons. They were too small for entire prints, and they'd been touched a lot, so mostly she just got static.

She did another check of the monitors. Still time. Still time. Rae rubbed her hands down her sides, trying to dry them from the beads of sweat forming on her palms. Then she ran her fingers over the buttons again, more slowly.

There isn't static on all of them, she realized. *Just on three, four, seven, and nine. Which means . . .*

Rae jabbed in the combo three, four, seven, nine. The door didn't open. *Okay, but there are only four numbers,* she thought. *That's not so many combos.*

As fast as she could, Rae punched in the numbers in a different order. No luck.

Will it only give me a certain number of tries before an alarm goes off? she wondered, her heart snaking its way up into her throat. *Got to risk it,* Rae decided, stabbing at the keypad. She swallowed hard, trying to get her heart back down where it was supposed to be, since it felt like it had almost blocked out her airflow. It didn't budge. She typed in another combo. The last one. And the door didn't open.

If she thought it would help, Rae would rip her throat open with her fingernails to get some air in. How was she supposed to think when she couldn't breathe?

You can breathe, she told herself. She sucked in a mouthful of air just to prove it. Then, using just one finger, she lightly touched each button again. Yeah, it was only three, four, seven, and nine with the static. But the static she picked up on number four was just the tiniest bit louder. So maybe it was a five-number combo, not a four number. Which meant more variations. A bunch more. Would she have time?

Rae punched in a five-number sequence with two fours in it, then cursed. She'd hit the two instead of the three. So of course the door stayed locked. *Concentrate,* she ordered herself. She entered a combo. The door stayed locked. Another. Still locked. Another.

And then she heard a click. A beautiful, beautiful sound. Gently, reverently, Rae turned the doorknob and pulled. The door swung open. She looked over her shoulder at the monitors. Her heart began to thud against the walls of her throat. Jesse and the rent-a-cop were in a hallway. Were they heading back toward her?

She couldn't leave now. She was too close. Rae scurried through the door. The room she found herself in wasn't any bigger than a closet. There was one table, one chair, one monitor.

Clenching her hands into fists at her sides, Rae forced herself to look right into the picture on the monitor. And her whole body stiffened. It looked exactly like a hospital unit. Four beds, and in the beds patients hooked up to IV drips and heart monitors and Rae wasn't sure what else. A woman with a clipboard moved from bed to bed, making notations.

"Experiments," Rae whispered. "They're still doing experiments in this place." What else could be happening in that room? It's not like the Wilton Center had a six-week course where you knitted a sweater and a six-week course where you became a doctor. *Was my mom ever in one of those beds?* she wondered. *Was Mandy's mom?* Hot bile splashed into Rae's throat, and she swallowed hard, trying to force it back down. It didn't work. She could still feel the sting of the acid. What exactly were they doing to those people?

Think about it later. It's time to get out of here, Rae told herself. She slipped back into the main security room, careful to shut the door behind her, then darted into the hall. A second later Jesse and the rent-a-cop rounded the corner, heading back for the security room. The rent-a-cop looked . . . not so happy.

I'm going in, Rae thought, hoping the rent-a-cop hadn't registered the fact that he and Jesse had passed by her on their way out. "There you are," she cried, rushing toward them. "I've been looking all over the place. Mom's already in the parking lot."

"I think you should ask your mother to come inside," the rent-a-cop told Rae.

"Why? What happened? Is something wrong?" Rae asked.

Jesse shot her a calm-down-already look, but Rae thought slightly hysterical was the way to go.

"What happened is that your brother here told me when he was in the bathroom, he saw a gun in another kid's backpack," the rent-a-cop answered. "But not only did we not find the kid, it took your brother quite a while to find the bathroom he supposedly had been in right before he came to get me. He said it was because he was nervous, but—" He stopped, shaking his head.

Obviously our plan had a hole, Rae thought. *Should have found a bathroom first. Okay, time to see if we can recover.* She took a step closer to the rent-a-cop, and his eyes did a fast—so fast, you could hardly see it—sweep over her enhanced breasts. *Good. Ick, but good,* Rae thought. She and Jesse would take any kind of advantage they could get.

"Here's the situation," Rae told him. She lowered her voice a little. "You know how there keep being those stories on the news about a kid going psycho at a school and blowing people away?" Rae continued on without waiting for an answer. "Well, it's completely disturbed my brother. I mean, he has nightmares almost every night. His room is across from mine, and the screams—God, I wake up with my heart going a million miles an hour." She moved a step closer, lowered her voice a little more. "He's even started wetting the bed. I'm sure he wasn't trying to jerk you around. He just gets scared sometimes, you know?"

"All right. Go on. Get out of here." The rent-a-cop turned to Jesse. "Next time be a lot more sure of what you saw."

"He will," Rae answered for Jesse. She grabbed him by the elbow, turned him around, and tugged him down the hall.

"I can't believe you said I wet the bed," Jesse muttered.

"Hey, it got us out of here, didn't it?" Rae answered as they headed out the main exit.

"Yeah, but it's not like it's the *only* thing you could have said," Jesse complained. "So what'd you find out?"

Rae filled him in as they cut across the parking lot and started down the sidewalk toward the bus stop.

"We should start working on a plan to get ourselves into that room and—" Jesse broke off abruptly. "Anything seem strange to you about that blue van across the street?"

"Like that it's going extremely slowly," Rae answered, struggling not to stare at the van with the tinted windows.

"Yeah. And that it's staying almost right across from us," Jesse said.

Without consulting each other, they both passed the bus stop and made a right at the closest corner. "Is it still there?" Rae forced the words through her sandpaper throat.

"Yeah," Jesse answered. And they both began to

run. Rae heard the van pick up speed behind them. A rushing sound filled her ears as she pushed herself to go faster, pumping her arms and legs.

"At the corner fake like you're going right," Jesse called. "When they start to turn, we'll cut—"

It took Rae several feet to realize Jesse was no longer beside her. She skidded to a stop and spun around to face him. He lay on the sidewalk, eyes staring straight up, his mouth open wide enough to show his lolling tongue.

"Oh, God. Oh, no." Rae bolted over and fell to her knees next to Jesse. She slapped him lightly on the face. "Jesse, come on, talk to me." He didn't move.

Her hand trembling, Rae felt his neck for a pulse. Her fingers brushed against something sharp, and she looked down. It took her brain a moment to process what she was seeing.

A tranquilizer dart.

Chapter 8

Anthony wandered through the mall. He hated malls. All malls. He hated shopping. But he wanted to get Rae a good birthday present for tomorrow night, something to make her . . . well, he just wanted to get her something good. So he wouldn't look like an idiot with her dad there and all.

He passed The Body Shop, hesitated, then turned around and stepped inside. There were bottles of who knew what everywhere, way too many bottles. On tables. On shelves. On counters. If he made one wrong move, he could smash half a dozen of them at a shot. Carefully Anthony picked up a squat glass jar of something called a sugar scrub. Sixteen bucks. So if he knocked over a table, it would cost him—

"Those brown-sugar scrubs are amazing," a salesclerk with her hair in ponytails gushed as she headed up to him. "They exfoliate all the dead skin cells, and they hold the moisture in. They come in vanilla, lavender, Indian gardenia, and citrus."

Citrus. Rae'd like that. It would go with that perfume she already wore. Suddenly Anthony's mind got very busy imagining Rae in the shower, rubbing the sugar stuff over—

Crap. What was he—crap. Anthony slammed the jar back down, setting the other jars rattling.

"Not what you were looking for, huh?" the ponytailed salesclerk said, pushing one of the jars away from the edge of the table.

"No." Anthony ran his fingers over his face. "No," he said again.

"You looking for a present? We have lots of other nice stuff," the salesclerk told him. "There are these wonderful cocoa butter moisturizers." She picked up a large, round tin. Anthony tried to look at it, but it went silvery and blurry. All he could think about was Rae smoothing on—

"No," Anthony burst out, backing out of the store. "No, thanks." He tore off. He didn't slow down until he got to a bookstore. *Okay,* he thought. *This is good. I can get her an art book. A nice one.*

Expensive. He had some money from the car repair jobs he got every once in a while.

By the time he found the art section, his pits were damp. Too many books in this place. Too many people who actually liked to read. *Just pick one and get out,* he told himself. Except how was he supposed to pick? Even in this one section there were hundreds of books. What if he chose the wrong one, one about an artist everyone knew sucked? He'd look like a moron.

"What am I doing in here?" Anthony muttered. He jammed his hands in his pockets and made his way toward the door, weaving between the rows and rows of books.

Now what? he asked himself when he was out in the mass of shoppers circling the mall's walkways. He wasn't ready to go back in another store. Not until his sweat production had gone down a couple of notches. Instead he wandered over to one of the little carts that circled the biggest fountain. A bunch of necklaces were laid out on a white cloth. Anthony liked them. They were delicate; that's what he guessed you'd call it. The silver chains were so thin, they were almost invisible, so the little charm things would look like they were kind of hovering over the girl's skin.

Anthony picked one up, his hands feeling big and

beefy. He liked the sparkly blue flower charm. The color was pretty much exactly the same blue as Rae's eyes. He checked the price tag. Not anywhere near cheap. But he could cover it. And it'd be worth it to get Rae something she'd really like.

"Your girlfriend will love it," the cart guy said, as if he could read Anthony's mind.

"It's not for my girlfriend," Anthony answered.

The cart guy winked. "If she's not, she will be when you give her that."

Anthony dropped the necklace back on the cloth. *The guy's right,* he thought. You only gave a girl a present like this if you were hoping to get together with her. Like Marcus giving Rae the freakin' bracelet, or trying to.

He hurried away from the cart. "You're not going to find anything better," the guy called after him. Anthony didn't look back. He walked straight into the closest store. *I'm buying something here,* he promised himself. *Something that says friend. Something I could give to Jesse.*

Rae ripped the tranquilizer dart out of Jesse's neck, getting a tiny fragment of a thought that she couldn't decipher. She carefully placed it in her jacket pocket. Then everything began to move in slow motion. Her thoughts. Her movements. The beat of her heart.

The van? Where's the . . . blue van? Her head came up, slowly, slowly, and she saw the van gliding to a stop in the street alongside them. Each time her slow, strong heart moved, it rocked her chest. Ba . . . boom. Ba . . . boom.

"Jesse! Jesse, you've got to get up," Rae cried. It felt like it took an eternity for the words to leave her lips. Jesse's eyes stared up at her face, but she knew he didn't see her, didn't see anything.

Ba . . . boom. Ba . . . boom. Under the sound of her thudding heart, Rae heard a clicking sound. She risked another look at the van and saw the side door begin to slide open.

"Help!" Rae screamed as loud as she could. She pushed one hand under Jesse's back and shoved him away from the sidewalk. At the same time she grabbed the front of his shirt with her free hand and pulled. Slowly, much too slowly, she managed to get Jesse to his feet. "Heeeelp!" she screamed again, the inside of her throat feeling like it was shredding as the word came out and out and out.

Rae started up the lawn of the closest house, dragging Jesse with her. She kept her eyes locked on the house's lime green door. Each step seemed to take an entire minute. Ba . . . boom. Ba . . . boom. Her heart was beating so slowly, Rae was sure it would stop. Where were . . . the people . . .

from the van? she thought, her brain in lowest gear.

She expected to feel a hand grab her shoulder. Or a dart pierce her back. Just . . . run, she told herself. Keep . . . going. She struggled forward, feeling like she was fighting her way through sticky oatmeal. Ba . . . boom. Ba . . . boom. Jesse collapsed to his knees. Rae didn't take the time to get him onto his feet again. She hunched over, tightened her grip on him, and yanked him across the lawn, the lawn made of oatmeal. It sucked at her feet with each step.

The lime green door didn't seem any closer than it had before. Ba . . . boom. Ba . . . boom. Rae fought her way toward it. *I have . . . to be closer,* she thought. Then the door flew open.

Baboombaboombaboom. Rae's heart spasmed against her ribs. Time was moving at normal speed again. No, superspeed.

A short woman appeared in the doorway. "What's-goingon?" she yelled.

Rae didn't understand what the woman had said. It was too fast, too jumbled. "You'vegottohelpus," Rae shouted, jerking Jesse toward the woman. "They'reafterus." Even her own words came out sounding scrambled.

As soon as the woman saw Jesse, she flew down the steps. She wrapped one arm around Jesse's shoulders, and the world returned to normal speed.

"Who's after you?" the woman exclaimed.

Rae shot a glance over her shoulder. The van was gone. "Doesn't matter. We need to call nine-one-one. I don't know if he's still breathing." She and the woman managed to get Jesse up the two porch steps, into the house, and over to the couch. "Please, you've got to get help. He, I don't know, he might be dying."

The woman nodded and rushed out of the room. Rae lowered her head to Jesse's chest. Oh, God, oh, thank God. His heart was still beating. She hadn't been sure. She'd been afraid he was already gone. "It's going to be okay, Jesse. You're going to be okay." She pressed her ear to his chest again. Just to be sure.

Rae lifted her head when she heard footsteps rushing back into the room. "The paramedics are on their way," the woman said. For the first time Rae really looked at her. She was younger than Rae expected, twentyish, with short black hair. "How's he doing?"

"He's breathing," Rae answered. "I think—" The inside of her nose began to prickle, and a lump the size of an egg formed in her throat.

"The paramedics are going to be here any minute," the woman said, clearly realizing Rae was about to lose it. "What happened out there?"

Not the time for the truth, Rae thought. If she told this woman the truth, maybe someday the people in the van would come back to this house, break in, and kill the woman in her own bed. The thought made her shudder. "There were these guys, these older guys, like in college, in a convertible. They were following us, driving really slow, you know. They started yelling stuff at us. Then one of them threw a bottle. We started to run, and Jesse—" Rae swallowed the salty egg lump that kept re-forming in her throat. "Jesse, he collapsed."

Rae reached out and stroked Jesse's cheek with the back of her knuckles. Then she moved her hand over a little, wanting to feel his breath, wanting proof that—

Jesse coughed, and Rae let out a little squeak. His eyelids fluttered, then opened. *He can see me,* Rae realized. It was impossible to miss the awareness in his blue eyes. "What happened?" he mumbled.

A sound that was half laugh, half sob came out of Rae. "I'll go stand out front and flag down the paramedics," the woman said. Rae nodded. She didn't think she could speak right now.

"What happened?" Jesse asked again after the woman left.

Rae cleared her throat. "Tranquilizer dart from our friends in the van," she told him, trying to keep her voice steady. A siren began to wail, coming closer every second. Quickly Rae told Jesse the cover story she'd given to the woman.

Jesse sat up. "Let's get out of here."

The siren grew louder and then stopped. "Too late," Rae told him. "And I want them to look at you. Make sure you're okay."

"I'm fine," Jesse protested, but Rae had caught the little wince as he raised his head all the way. "My arm's kind of messed up, but I'm fine."

"You don't know that," Rae shot back. Before he could answer, the paramedics dashed into the room. Rae stood up and backed away from the couch to give them room. They asked Jesse what happened, and he parroted back the cover story. Then they listened to his heart, took his blood pressure, checked his pupils.

"Pressure's a little low," one of the paramedics said. "So's the heart rate. Low, but okay."

"Then can I go?" Jesse demanded.

"He said his arm hurt," Rae jumped in. Jesse scowled at her, but she didn't care. She wanted the paramedics to check him out completely.

"Can you move your fingers?" the paramedic who'd taken his blood pressure asked.

"Yeah." Jesse wiggled his fingers, and Rae could see he was struggling not to grimace.

"Bend your elbow for me," the same paramedic said, running his fingers up and down Jesse's arm. "Looks like you got off with some scrapes and bruises," the paramedic told Jesse.

"Like I said, I'm fine. Now can I go home?" Jesse snapped.

The paramedic glanced over at the woman whose house they were in. "I think it would be—"

"I'm not related to him," the woman interrupted. "I don't want to make any decisions."

"Is one of your parents at home now?" the paramedic asked Jesse.

"My mom should be," Jesse answered.

"I think you're in good shape. But I want to take you home, talk to your mom," the paramedic told Jesse. "She should bring you in to your own doctor so you can find out what could have caused the collapse."

"If you drive up to my house in an ambulance, you're going to have to take my mom away in it. She'll freak," Jesse said in a rush.

"We won't use the siren. We'll be low-key," the paramedic promised.

"I'm coming, too," Rae announced.

A couple of minutes later they were on the road. Rae couldn't stop staring at Jesse. She needed to keep reassuring herself that he was really okay.

"Would you stop it?" he complained. "You're creeping me out."

"Sorry," Rae mumbled. She folded her hands and stared down at them, only sneaking peeks at Jesse when she absolutely had to to keep her sanity.

"You're going to have to help me calm down my mom," Jesse told Rae as they turned onto his street. "Siren or not, she's going to lose it."

Rae nodded. The ambulance pulled to a stop. Rae could hear Mrs. Beven screaming before the paramedics got the back doors open. The high sound penetrated Rae's bones, chilling them.

"Mom, I'm okay. I'm fine. Look at me. I'm fine," Jesse said as soon as the back doors opened and he could see his mother.

Mrs. Beven scrambled into the ambulance and wrapped her arms around Jesse. She started rocking him like he was a little baby. And Jesse let her.

She could have lost Jesse today, Rae thought. *And it would have been my fault.* She climbed out of the ambulance. It wasn't her place to be there. What Mrs. Beven was going through was too intimate for someone who was practically a stranger to see.

I'm not going to put him at risk again, Rae vowed. *I'm going after the killer myself. My life is the only one I'm going to put in danger.*

I'm the one the killer is after. I'm not putting anybody else in his path. Not again. Absently she rubbed her side where the most recent numb spot had been. *And anyway, there's not as much the killer can do to me. I could be dying already.*

Rae heard the driver's-side door of Aiden Matthews's car open. She pressed herself tighter against the floor of the backseat.

"I know you're there," Aiden said, sounding perfectly calm. "I figured you'd be the type to come back instead of using the system I came up with for you to contact me. That's why I left the pillow and blanket back there. God knows what you would have done if I'd decided to be smart and locked the car." He slammed the door and started the engine. "Stay down. I'll find us a place to talk."

Rae didn't want to stay down. She wanted to hurl herself into the front seat and scream at Aiden until her face turned purple. She wanted to hit him until he was black and blue. He knew who had shot that tranquilizer dart at Jesse. Rae was sure of that. He knew everything. The truth about her mother. The truth about whoever was trying to kill Rae. And today he was going to tell it to her.

She closed her eyes and relaxed her fisted hands. *Wait until we get . . . wherever,* she told herself.

Don't be stupid. The car could be being watched right now.

After what felt like forever, Aiden pulled the car to a stop. He got out without a word. Rae scrambled out after him and followed him into a run-down coffee shop. He took a seat in the back booth. Rae slid onto the padded bench across from him, her muscles tight after hiding in the car for so long.

Aiden put a quarter in the little jukebox. He didn't speak until some ancient tune began to play. "Do you know how dangerous it is for you to get as close to the center as you did? The parking lot is—"

"You want to know what dangerous is?" Rae interrupted, her voice as low as his had been. Rae slammed the tranquilizer dart down onto the table in front of him. "Dangerous is getting shot in the neck with one of these darts, like some kind of freaking animal. Which is what happened to my friend Jesse today because he, unlike *you*, was willing to help me." She pulled in a long, jagged breath. "I want you to tell me everything you know."

Aiden carefully picked up the dart, turned it over in his fingers, then wrapped it in a napkin from the metal dispenser and pushed it back toward Rae. "I want to help you. But telling you anything is not—" Aiden began.

"Are you willing to be responsible for my

death?" Rae demanded. "Because if you're not, you should start talking."

Aiden gave his ridiculous little ponytail a tug. He closed his eyes for a long moment, then opened them, reached into his jacket pocket, and pulled out a fistful of change. He fed every quarter he had into the jukebox. "Here's what I know," he said. "I'll start at the beginning."

Rae nodded. "You know your mother was in a group at the Wilton Center before you were born." Rae nodded again. "The purpose of the group was to enhance the psychic powers of people who had already shown an above-average amount of intuitive ability."

"Shown how?" Rae asked. A waitress brought over two glasses of water, and Rae gulped hers down.

"What can I get you?" the waitress asked.

"Coffee," Aiden answered.

"Me, too," Rae said. All she wanted was for the waitress to get away.

"Be right back." The waitress walked off, her pink sneakers squeaking on the linoleum floor.

"Go on," Rae urged, gripping the edge of the table—

/**starving**/*no one will see*/**got to**/**love that song**/

—to keep herself from reaching over and shaking

Aiden. "You were going to explain the intuitive-ability thing."

"The scientist who ran the group did some tests. Basic things," Aiden told her. "Having the prospective members predict which card would be the next one to come up in the deck. Pairing them up and having one person draw an object while the other one tried to guess what it was."

"I get it," Rae said, not wanting to waste a second. "And my mom was good at this stuff?"

"Above average. Like everyone who was let into the group," Aiden answered. The waitress squeaked over with their coffee, then squeaked away.

"And the enhancing part. What exactly does that mean? What did the *scientist* do to them?" Rae asked.

Aiden ripped open a packet of sugar and put it in his coffee. Then he ripped open another. And another. *Does he even realize what he's doing?* Rae wondered when he'd emptied five of the packets into his cup. She reached over and grabbed his wrist. "Enough. Keep talking."

"There were various methods." Aiden took a long sip on his coffee, then grimaced, as if he was surprised by the taste. "Various drugs, electric stimulation, radiation. At the time I wasn't kept completely informed. I was just out of college and—"

"I'm not interested in your life story," Rae snapped, her mind stuck on the phrase *electric stimulation*. Had her mother gotten electric shock? Had she been tied down and—

"The response in some of the group members, including your mother, was astonishing. The psychic powers that some of them developed were tremendous. The group was shut down until the results could be fully evaluated. There was a fear—" Aiden put another packet of sugar into his coffee. "There was a fear that some of the members had developed powers that were too strong to be controlled. You have to understand, if these powers were used irresponsibly or for personal gain, it could be a threat to our society. On the scale of a nuclear weapon in some cases."

Aiden hesitated. Rae noticed that there were dark smudges under his eyes. He looked exhausted. But she didn't care. "Keep going," she ordered.

"The scientist who ran the group disappeared. There was speculation that he felt tremendous guilt for having designed the enhancement techniques. Especially when the murders began."

"Murders?" Rae's coffee cup clattered against the saucer as she picked it up. She ended up pretending to take a sip. Her hands were shaking too much for her to be sure that she'd get the liquid into her mouth.

"Murders of members of the group. The administrators of the program believed that the scientist was responsible. That he wanted to eliminate any possible danger to—"

"By killing," Rae interrupted.

"Yes," Aiden said, meeting her gaze straight on.

"Who are the administrators?" Rae asked. "I want to meet them."

"No," Aiden told her, his voice filled with determination. "That's impossible. You have to leave this alone, Rae. I won't be able to protect you if you don't."

"You have to answer one more question," Rae told him.

"No. I've said too much already. Everything you hear puts you in more danger." Aiden stood up.

"The disease my mom died of—the wasting disease. I'm afraid maybe I have it," Rae blurted. "Maybe what they did to her screwed up her genes."

Aiden sank back down in the booth. He reached out to her, as if he was going to take both her hands in his, then he grabbed his coffee cup with both his hands instead. "No, Rae, you don't have to worry about that. Believe me."

"Why should I?" she asked, hating the way her voice had begun to tremble.

"Because your mother didn't die of a disease. Steve Mercer—" He stopped abruptly.

He didn't mean to say that name, Rae realized. "Steve Mercer? Who's Steve Mercer?" she demanded.

Aiden let out a sigh. "He's the man who killed her," Aiden answered. He pushed the napkin holder closer to her, using the back of his hand. She shoved it away. She felt like she'd been hit on the head by a baseball bat. Little dots of light were exploding in front of her eyes.

"Steve Mercer? Steve Mercer?" All she could do was say the name.

"The scientist," Aiden explained. "The administrators believe that he got into her hospital room and injected her with a compound that turned her body against itself. I know . . . I can imagine how horrible it is for you to hear this. But it was murder, Rae. It's nothing that you've inherited."

"Except that someone has tried to kill me more than once," Rae said. She squeezed the edge of the table until her fingers ached. "It's him, isn't it? It's Steve Mercer?"

"Very likely," Aiden admitted. His eyes darted around the restaurant, and Rae noticed that droplets of sweat had broken out on his upper lip. She pushed the napkin holder back toward him.

"And the *administrators,* they just sit there and

do nothing?" Rae shook her head, and more bursts of color exploded in front of her eyes.

"They're going to find him, Rae. They're going to take him down. I promise you that." Aiden wiped the sweat off his lip with his fingers. The droplets immediately re-formed.

"You promise. You make too many promises," Rae muttered. "I want to talk to them myself. You've got to get me to them."

"The administrators have more power than almost anyone in the country," Aiden said, his voice cold. Hard. He leaned across the table toward her, getting right in her face. "They're government, okay? And Rae, listen to me, if you get in their way at all, they won't hesitate to kill you themselves."

Chapter 9

"The place doesn't seem that fancy," Anthony commented as Yana pulled up in front of the Nacoochee Grill. It looked more like a house than a restaurant, a big white house with a tin roof and a wide front porch.

"Yeah, and you're an expert in fine dining, right?" Yana snapped as she parked. "Everyone knows this place is amazing. Rae's daddy isn't going to bring his little girl anywhere but the best for her birthday."

Yana definitely had her bitch juice this morning, Anthony thought. Most of the time when she got sarcastic, it was funny. But not today. He unbuckled his seat belt and opened the car door. Yana snagged him by the arm before he could get out. "We're early.

151

We're supposed to get to the table with the dessert."

"Right." Anthony slammed the door shut. Yana didn't let go of his arm.

"Sorry I've been a buzz kill tonight." She fluffed her white-blond hair, checked herself out in the vanity mirror on the visor, and then sighed. "I'm just nervous about seeing Rae."

"Me, too. Sort of," Anthony admitted.

"You didn't have a massive fight with her," Yana said.

Yeah, but I kissed her, Anthony thought. *And I don't think I've actually looked her in the eye since then.* Kissed. What a stupid little word. What he and Rae had done . . . it should be called something else. Something more awesome. And now, he thought as he checked the clock on the dashboard, in less than half an hour he was going to be sitting near her, maybe near enough to smell that citrus stuff she wore, and—

No. What's going to happen is that you're going to be sitting near Yana, Anthony corrected himself. *And you're going to be showing Rae that you and Yana are together and that the three of you can all play nice and be friends. Then pretty soon Rae will end up with Marcus or some guy like Marcus, some guy who's smart and fits in and everything, and the four of you will then all be best friends forever.*

The thought of being with Rae and some other guy, having to watch them—Anthony gave his head a hard shake, wanting to hurl the image out of his brain.

"What?" Yana asked.

Anthony cracked his knuckles, then cracked them again. "Nothing. I just want to get this over with."

"It's going to be fine," Yana told him, running her fingers through his hair. "She's going to be glad to see us, and we're going to have fun. We'll make it a birthday Rae will never forget."

Rae took another bite of her grilled vegetables. She knew she loved them. She always ordered them here because at Nacoochee, they cooked everything over big fire pits and the veggies got all smoky and yummy. But tonight, God, she could be eating dog biscuits. It was like every part of her brain—even the part that usually relayed info from her taste buds—was focused on what Aiden had told her.

I have to go after Steve Mercer, she thought for probably the billionth time. *If I don't, he's going to kill me. And the administrators, from whatever part of the government they're from, they might not move fast enough to save me. If they'd even want to. They sure didn't protect my mother, or Mandy's mother, or any of those people from the group I wasn't able to track down.* Rae shuddered, imagining all of them in a pile, a pile of corpses.

"Are you cold?" her father asked.

"No. Just—" Rae shrugged. "Some weird muscle spasm." She forced herself to smile at him. It was so clear he wanted this birthday to be special. Rae could give him that, couldn't she? The illusion of a perfect sixteenth birthday, the illusion of a normal, happy daughter.

"Sixteen. Hard to believe you're sixteen," her dad said, his eyes moist with emotion.

Rae felt her own eyes tear up. *If Steve Mercer had his way, I'd be dead by now,* she thought. *My dad would be all alone, his whole family murdered.*

But if I can find a way to stop Mercer, then everything is okay again, Rae reminded herself. She gave a couple of hard blinks to get the tears out of her eyes. *There's not some disease growing in me. By my next birthday, if I manage to come up with a plan that works, I won't have to be pretending to be happy. I'll be alive. And no one will be after me.*

I'll be alive! The thought was like drinking champagne, which she'd done a couple of times at weddings. It made her feel all fizzy inside.

She smiled at her father. "So, am I what you thought I'd be like? I mean, when I was little, did you ever try to imagine how I'd turn out?" Rae asked.

"Actually, no, I didn't try to picture what you'd be like at some other age." Her father picked up the last piece of corn bread and held it out to her. She shook her head, and he started to butter the bread. "I was always too interested in whatever you were right at the moment."

Rae speared the last piece of vegetable on her plate, glad she'd made it through without choking. *If you feel like you're going to gag during cake, just remember the good news Aiden gave you. No disease. No disease!*

"Like when I taught you how to ride a bike," her father continued. He paused to take a bite of his bread.

"The bike story again?" Rae complained. But she was glad he'd decided to drag it out. Maybe it would help to hear it again.

"One of my favorites," he answered. "You fell down I don't know how many times that day. Your knees got all skinned up. I was starting to think—"

"That I'd have to ride a tricycle the rest of my life," Rae jumped in.

"Well, it was looking likely," her dad answered. He reached across the table and pushed a section of her curly hair away from her face. "But you kept getting back on. You were determined. I was afraid you'd scrape off every inch of skin before you were done. But finally you got on the bike again, I gave you a push, and you rode. You rode. So even though I didn't spend a lot of time wondering what you'd end up like, I knew you'd be able to do pretty much anything you wanted. Because you'd keep trying no matter what."

Rae'd hoped hearing the story again would leave her pumped up—ready to face Steve Mercer and anybody else. Instead she just felt wistful and nostalgic. God, if only her biggest problem was trying to ride a two-wheeler. If only her dad could still be there to give her a push and cheer her on.

"Can I take this away?" a voice asked from behind her.

Rae jerked her head toward the voice, heart thundering. It was the waiter. Of course it was just the waiter. But she hadn't even heard him come up. That wasn't good. She had to be able to sense someone approaching. She had to feel it when someone was watching her from afar. "Sure. Thanks," she answered, when she realized the waiter was still waiting for an answer.

"You can take mine, too," Rae's father said. "It was magnificent."

"Yeah, everything was great," Rae added quickly.

Was she pulling this off? She shot a look at her dad. Did he have any clue that most of the time only her body had been in the restaurant with him while her mind was off plotting and planning, concocting how she could free herself of Steve Mercer? He didn't seem to. Her dad seemed like he was having a perfect night.

"It's that time," he said.

"Huh?" she asked. Before he could answer, she'd figured it out because a group of waiters had started to sing "Happy Birthday." A second later most of the other diners had joined in.

Rae felt the warmth of a blush seeping into her cheeks. This always happened to her, every birthday. When the singing started, she blushed. She felt like covering her head with a napkin, but because she was sixteen and not four, she turned toward the waiters moving toward her with a jumbo butterscotch brownie alight with candles and gave her best fake smile.

"Oh, my God," she cried when she saw who was behind the waiters. Yana was here. And so was Anthony. She froze, staring at their expressions. What were they doing here? Had her dad guilted them into this? God, how completely humiliating. But as the panic started to fade, she realized that they were both smiling. Real smiles. Like they actually *wanted* to be here.

Her zirconium smile turned to real diamond. Anthony and Yana's smiles turned to grins.

Looks like Yana's definitely forgiven me, Rae thought with a rush of warmth. *Maybe Anthony talked her into it.* Who cared how it happened? They were both here. And all her angry, bitter feelings toward both of them had evaporated, leaving her feeling clean and birthday happy inside. She turned to her dad. "You did this, didn't you?" she asked. He nodded, without stopping singing. "Thanks." She leaned across the table and kissed his cheek. "Thanks, thanks, thanks."

One of the waiters set the massive sundae down in front of her. A second later Yana was leaning down to hug her. "Happy birthday, Rae," Anthony said.

"Sit down, you guys, sit down," Rae urged Anthony and Yana. "You've got to help us eat this massive thing."

"That's the plan," Anthony told her. He plopped down in one of the chairs the waiters had brought over and grabbed a spoon. Rae's heart felt like it had been turned into a bubble machine. All these light, happy bubbles were swirling around inside her. And she couldn't stop smiling. Even if she used her fingers to pull down the corners of her mouth, she wouldn't be able to stop. Anthony and Yana were here!

"Remember to make a wish," Yana said. She took the seat next to Anthony as Rae prepared to blow out the candles.

Some of the happy bubbles popped as she realized that she had only one wish. *I wish Steve Mercer was dead,* Rae thought. She sucked in a deep breath, so deep, her lungs ached in protest, then blew out all the candles with a whoosh. Her dad, Anthony, Yana, and the waiters all clapped.

"You can't tell anybody what it was," her dad reminded her with a wink. "Or it won't come true."

A few more of the happy bubbles popped. That wasn't the only reason she couldn't tell her wish. It was life threatening to everybody who heard it.

Rae shoved the sundae into the center of the table. "Go for it, everybody," she said, digging her spoon into one corner of the brownie where the butterscotch sauce was especially thick. *For one hour you can be here with your dad and your friends and your favorite dessert and pretend nothing else in the world exists,* she told herself. *Nothing else and no one else.* She slid her spoon into her mouth, savoring the warmth and gooey sweetness of the sauce. *For just this hour, on your birthday, your life can be this perfect.*

"Is it good?" Anthony asked, spoon poised over the brownie.

"It's the best thing you've ever tasted," Rae promised him. God, she'd missed him. Him and Yana, too.

Anthony flicked a birthday candle out of the way, then dug a chunk out of the brownie with his spoon. "The best, yeah," he mumbled after he popped the brownie into his mouth.

"It does look fantastic," Yana commented. Then she leaned close to Anthony, wiped a glob of butterscotch off his cheek with her napkin, and gave the newly clean spot a little kiss.

They're . . . they're together, Rae realized.

The happy bubbles inside her burst, all of them, all at once. They left behind an oily residue that coated Rae inside, covering her brain and her heart and her lungs, coating her throat with a rotten taste. A dead taste.

I can't be here. I can't, she thought. Rae used both hands to push herself up from the table, her wax-coated fingers preventing her from picking up any thoughts. "Be right back," she managed to say, even though her tongue felt thick with the rancid oil.

The oil sloshed inside her as she walked to the bathroom. The first thing she did was dig in her purse for some mints. She had to get the dead taste out of her mouth. Finally she found two wintergreen

Certs. She threw them into her mouth and chewed them hard. It didn't help.

"Rae, I have a question for you."

Rae jerked her head toward the voice, oil churning in her mouth, sloshing into her heart. Yana half sat, half leaned on the first sink in the row. "I just want to know how it feels to have your best friend go behind your back," she continued. "I mean, I know how it felt when you did it to me. But now that it's your turn, what's it like?"

Yana drove past Anthony's house and parked half a block down. He knew what that meant. She wanted to make out. Yeah, here came her hands, wrapping themselves in his hair, pulling his face to hers.

Anthony's body responded on autopilot, his lips meeting hers. But it was like he'd been shot up with novocaine. He could feel a little pressure, knew in his head what was happening, but that was it.

It was because Rae's face, Rae's face in that second she realized he and Yana were together, wouldn't get out of his brain. She hadn't just been surprised. She'd been in pain. Anthony and Yana had hurt her.

What was he thinking, going in there with Yana without giving Rae any kind of warning? he asked himself. Parked out in front of the restaurant, he'd been thinking about just how much torture it would be to see Rae with another guy. But he hadn't thought Rae would feel that way. Because that would mean—

Yana gave Anthony's lip a not-too-gentle bite. "What?" he protested.

"I just wanted to make sure you were still alive," she told him. Automatically he put his hands on her waist, then leaned in and deepened the kiss.

The image of Rae's face shrank. But it didn't disappear.

just want to know how it feels to have your best friend go behind your back.

"I have one more birthday surprise for you," Rae's father said as he unlocked the front door.

If you get in their way at all, they won't hesitate to kill you themselves. . . . I'll talk to her for you. . . . Drugs, electric stimulation, radiation.

"Surprise. Great," Rae answered as she followed him into the house.

"You go sit in the living room. I'll be right back," her dad told her.

Somehow Rae managed to follow the simple instruction. Then she realized her father was still standing in the same place, looking at her.

I just want to know how it feels to have your best

*friend go behind your back. . . . Steve Mercer? Steve
Mercer?*

*Can Dad tell I'm breaking apart? Is he trying to
decide if he should call Ms. Abramson?*

Her father gave a blink and shook his head. "I
was staring, wasn't I?"

*Stay away from places you don't belong. . . . What
are you most afraid of? . . . Cries watching* Frosty the
Snowman.

"Yeah," Rae answered, struggling to keep her
conversation with her father separate from the bab-
ble in her head.

"Sorry," her dad said. "It's just that I've been
waiting so long to give you this. I . . ." It was as if
his throat had gotten too clogged for him to speak.
He cleared it. "I . . . I guess I should just go get it.
That's probably the best way."

"Okay," Rae managed to answer. Her father
turned and headed out of the room, with one last
over-the-shoulder look at her.

*So, I gotta go. . . . I won't be able to protect you. . . .
Won't be able to protect your best friend . . . Why do
you keep talking about my mother? . . . Ashes to ashes.*

Rae folded her hands tightly in her lap. She knew
the thoughts slicing through her brain weren't coming from fingerprints. But that's how they felt. Alien.
Unwelcome.

Because your mother didn't die of a disease . . . I just want to know how it feels to have your best friend go behind your back. . . . How would you be most afraid to die?

"Stop it," Rae whispered. *Stop it.* This was like the day in the caf last spring. She was losing her mind. Any second now she'd be throwing things and screaming her guts out. And then she'd be back in her quiet room in the hospital.

It happened to Amanda. . . . It could happen to you. . . . Stay away from places you don't belong. . . . Who are the administrators? . . . I'll talk to her for you. . . . I have football. So, I gotta go.

"Please stop. Please, please stop. Just until I'm alone," Rae begged, even though there was no one to beg to. This was all happening inside her. There was no one to help. No one who *could* help.

But it was murder, Rae. . . . It happened to Amanda. It could happen to you. . . . I'll talk to her for you. . . . Don't have to keep up a front with me . . . Ashes to mother. Mother to ashes.

Faintly, under the sound of the voices in her head—Anthony's, Yana's, Aiden's, Marcus's, Mr. Jesperson's, Ms. Abramson's, her own—Rae heard her father approaching. *Shut up,* she silently screamed at the voices in her head. For just a couple of minutes she had to seem like a normal girl, a normal birthday girl. She wasn't putting her father through another round of madness. No way was she doing that.

Everything you hear puts you in more danger. . . . I have football. . . . Your mother didn't die of a disease behind your back. . . . I'll talk to her for you. . . . Jesse, he collapsed.

Rae's father returned with a small box wrapped in pink-polka-dot paper and sat down next to her on the sofa. He cradled the box in both hands, as if it were made of the thinnest glass imaginable. "This isn't—" He had to stop to clear his throat again. "This isn't from me. It's from your mother."

The voices in Rae's head grew high and shrill, ripping into her.

Mother didn't die of a disease. . . . So, gotta go . . . Steve Mercer? Steve Mercer? . . . How are you most afraid to die? . . . Best friend murders football . . . They'reafterus.

"From Mom?" Rae said. She winced at how loudly her voice came out. *Only you can hear the voices,* she reminded herself sharply. *You don't have to try and talk over them.*

"She even wrapped it herself. In the hospital," her father answered. "I wanted to help because . . ." His voice trailed off, and his eyes seemed to focus on something that wasn't there. *A memory,* Rae realized.

Her father shook his head. "But she insisted on doing it herself. For you."

Radiation . . . So, gotta go . . . Drugs . . . How it feels to have Jesse collapse . . . How it feels to keep up a front . . . Electric stimulation . . . Ashes, ashes, we all fall down.

Saint Mom again, Rae thought. *He always remembers her as a freakin' angel. But she murdered her best friend.* Rae opened her mouth to try to get that fact through her father's delusional head one last time. But she couldn't do it. She couldn't hurt him like that. Not after everything he'd gone through. With her mother. And with Rae herself. And also . . . somehow Rae couldn't quite muster her usual bitterness on the topic of her mother. Not after everything she'd been through lately.

"I—I . . ." Rae lowered her gaze to the carpet and focused on one little spot, trying to gain some control. "I'd rather open it in my room. Is that okay?"

Frosty's gotta go. . . . They're after us. . . . They won't hesitate to kill you themselves. . . . Happy birthday to you. . . . Happy birthday, dear Rae.

"Of course it's okay." Her father placed the little box in Rae's wax-covered fingers, gently, tenderly, almost reluctantly. "Maybe I should have waited and given it to you tomorrow. I didn't want to upset you on your birthday. It's just that it meant so much to your mother—"

Mother didn't die of a football. . . . ShhhKILLhhh . . . It happened to Jesse. . . . It happened to Frosty. . . . It happened to Amanda. . . . It happened to your mother.

Rae staggered to her feet. "You didn't ruin anything," she said, trying to act like the voices were just a really annoying song on the radio, something that had nothing to do with her. Trying to act like her father's insistence on seeing her mother as some kind of princess of light didn't make her want to scream.

ShhhKILLhhh. ShhhKILLhhh. ShhhKILLhhh. ShhhKILLhhh.

"It was a great birthday," she said, enunciating each word slowly and carefully. She kissed him on the bald spot he was growing on the top of his head. "See you in the morning."

"I love you," her dad called after her as she started out of the living room, placing her feet slowly and carefully.

"Me you too," Rae answered. God, she was starting to talk like the voices. They were infecting her.

I just want to know how it feels. . . . I just want to know how it feels . . . To have your best friend put you in danger . . . So, I gotta go.

One foot, the other foot, one foot, the other foot.

Deliberately, focusing as much as she was able, Rae made her way into her bedroom and closed the door behind her. Then she walked straight to her bed. She didn't bother trying to take off her clothes. Too many movements. Too much to try and do with the voices, the voices that were now howling for her attention.

Go behind your back . . . So, I gotta go . . . Happy birthday, dead Steve Mercer . . . The administrators collapsed . . . ShhhKILLhhh . . . This isn't from me. It's from your mother.

Cautiously, cautiously, as if she were an ancient woman with brittle bones that could snap at any second, Rae lay down on her bed. She pulled the edge of her comforter around her and rolled over once, twice, until she was wrapped in a tight cocoon. *I'm just going to be still until it's over,* she decided. She could hardly hear the thought over the cacophony in her head.

Drugs. Radiation . . . How are you most afraid to die? Who? Who? Who?

Rae closed her eyes. She took in the most shallow breaths she could. "Stay still," she whispered, scarcely moving her lips. "That's all you can do."

God, I actually fell asleep, Rae realized, cautiously cracking open her eyes. She held her body still, so still, her muscles ached. But she had to be sure. Rae let out a long, shaky sigh. The voices . . . they were gone. For now. At least for now.

Rae tried to sit up, then realized she was still rolled tightly in her comforter, arms pinned against her sides. She turned over twice, moving back toward the edge of the bed, and the comforter fell away. The first thing her eyes landed on was the pink-polka-dot box. Rae glanced at her clock radio. Not even ten-thirty. Still her birthday. This was the time to open the gift. She wasn't sure if she wanted to or not, but she felt like she should. Fate or whatever.

She sat up and crossed her legs underneath her, then rubbed her fingertips together until all the wax flaked away. If she was going to do this, she was going to do it all out. Rae picked up the box before she could change her mind and turned it over in her hands.

/will Rae appreciate/wish I could be there/think of me sometimes/should I wait/know how much I love/wish she could give/never know/

Rae felt this warm blossom of love grow inside her, growing bigger and bigger until it was outside and inside at the same time. Complete you're-my-baby-and-I'll-love-you-forever parent kind of love. From her dad. And from her mom. Tons of it from her mom. There were little tendrils of fear and apprehension, too, but the love overpowered all the other feelings.

Remember all that mom love comes from a mom who killed her best friend, Rae told herself. But God, who knew how much Steve Mercer and his experiments had changed her mother? A tiny bit of the anger that always came when she thought about what her mother had done faded.

Rae peeled off the tape and slid the box free from the paper. She opened the lid, getting another burst of thoughts and emotions, this time all from her mother. Mostly love again. But still with those bits of fear. She saw a folded piece of pink paper and removed it with the tips of her fingers, needing a break from the intensity of the feelings trapped in her mother's fingerprints, then opened it, still managing to avoid a fresh blast.

A letter. It was a letter from her mom. Rae squeezed her eyes shut, not daring to look at it. What would it say? How much would it hurt to read it?

You can't ignore it, Rae told herself. She forced her eyes back open. And began to read.

Dearest Rachel,
    In this box you will find a locket that was given to me on my sixteenth birthday. It was given to my mother on her sixteenth birthday,

too. And back and back. Your great-great-great-great grandmother was the first one to receive it, if you can believe that. I know I had trouble imagining that many greats when my mother gave it to me.

I can't even tell you how much I wish I was there with you on your sixteenth birthday. Not just to give you the locket, although it would have been so wonderful to continue the tradition, but because you're at an age where there are things you might need me for. Your father is a wonderful man, and I know he's been a wonderful dad to you. It would be impossible for him not to be. But you're changing so fast now, I bet, and some of the changes are things you might want to talk to a woman about. A mother. Your mother. It breaks my heart to know that I won't be there for you. But there's not much time left for me. In a few days I probably won't be strong enough to write at all.

Enough. That isn't what I wanted to say. I would tear this up and start again if I thought I could do better. There are things you've inherited from me, Rachel. My chin, I think. My hands. But there could be other things, things neither of us would have recognized when you were a little girl. Some of these things may be difficult for you to deal with on your own. Things that could be frightening.

If I can, Rachel, if there is any way, I'll watch you from wherever it is I end up, maybe on a cloud with a harp, maybe as particles of energy that somehow are drawn to you. I want to be with you if you need me. I want to protect you. And if I can't . . . if I can't, I'm sure that you'll be strong enough to protect yourself.

My pen is feeling heavier and heavier, and as much as I want to write pages and pages and pages, I can't. There's one other thing I want to tell you. I know by now you'll have heard the stories about me. You'll have heard that I was accused of killing Erika Keaton, my best friend. I know your father will have told you this many times by now, but I want you to hear it from me—I swear to you that I did not murder her. I never would have done anything to hurt Erika. Never. Please don't ever be afraid that you have the capacity to do such an evil thing within yourself because of what you've heard about me.

I wish I could tell you everything. I wish I could give you enough evidence to bury even the tiniest bit of doubt. But there are reasons . . . I can't bear the thought of somehow bringing danger to you and your father. Just believe me. I know it's asking too much of you—you won't even have the tiniest memory of me—but believe me, believe that your mother, although she's done many stupid things, could never be the murderer they called me. I couldn't defend myself because—

I have to stop now, my Rachel. Happiest of birthdays, my sweetheart. I love you now. I will love you always.

XXXOOO
Mom

Rae allowed the letter to flutter from her fingers. There was no way she could keep holding it, not with the sobs shaking her body. "Oh God, Mom," she choked out. "Are you there somewhere watching? Because if you are, I could really, really use some help."

She listened—felt—for an answer, even just a tiny flicker of response. But Rae got nothing. She was all alone. Without her mother. Without Anthony. Without Yana.

Rae cried until she felt hollowed out inside, hollowed out and strangely calm. Detached. As if she was a second Rae, looking at the Rae crumbled into a soggy ball on the bed. She had to be logical, to think clearly. She had to make sense of all this.

Okay, first thing to do is see if Mom was telling the truth, Rae told her soggy self. She sat up, grabbed her mother's letter, and did a thorough fingerprint sweep.

/never hurt Erika/will Rachel have/can't tell/hurts/I won't be/heavy, so heavy/Rachel/Rachel/

A geyser of elation went off inside Rae. There was nothing in her mother's thoughts that indicated she was lying. If she had killed Erika, a thought about the murder would have had to have gone through her mother's head while she was touching the paper. Her mother couldn't write about being innocent without some little piece of a lie slipping out in her thoughts if she was actually guilty.

"I'm not the daughter of a murderer," Rae said aloud. It was so strange to hear the words. For so many years the fact that her mother had killed someone had felt like the most important thing about Rae. The thing she had to keep hidden. The thing that would make people recoil from her if they learned the truth.

Wait, Rae ordered herself. *Wait. Maybe Mom*

really believed she was innocent. But that doesn't mean she actually was. The experiments, the disease, either one could have affected her mind to the point that she couldn't separate reality from fantasy.

But Dad wasn't experimented on. Dad wasn't sick. And Rae had never gotten a splinter of a doubt in any of his thoughts about her mother. He loved her so much, Rae thought. He could just be delusional, not want to face the truth. That's what Rae had always believed.

Yet now . . . Wasn't there as much reason to believe her father—and her mother—were telling the truth? The idea that her mom had been framed for murder didn't seem nearly so delusional as it used to. The past months had shown Rae that a lot of stuff that seemed ridiculous and impossible was actually true and real. And she certainly knew what it was like to be afraid to let the people she cared about know the full truth—afraid that it would just put them in danger as well.

Rae took the locket out of the box, her eyes stinging at the rush of Mom emotion, and found the tiny mechanism that opened it. Inside was a picture of her mother. Her mother with really bad helmet hair, all poofy and hair-sprayed on top and the bangs, with the rest falling to her shoulders. Rae let out a choked laugh. "You look good, anyway, Mom," she said. She moved her eyes to the picture opposite her mother's, assuming she'd see a picture of her dad. Instead it was one of Rae's baby pictures. Rae's heart twisted up so tightly, she felt like it could spring out of her body.

"Maybe I'm joining Dad in the fantasy zone, but I believe you," she whispered, tears forming in her eyes. "I just do."

I'm never taking this off, Rae thought as she fastened the locket around her neck. *When I take Steve Mercer down, I'm going to be wearing it. Because we both deserve revenge. Me and my mom.*

Rae stood up and moved in front of her dresser. She wanted to see the locket on. But a flash of light distracted her. Headlights. Headlights of a car pulling into *her* driveway.

"Is that you, Mercer?" Rae muttered. "Because tonight I'm ready for you." She took a step toward the door, then froze. What was she thinking? She wasn't some kind of Terminator. She was just a girl, a girl who could read thoughts from fingerprints. There was no way she could march out there and take down a full-grown man. A man who very likely had a gun. *For God's sake, you almost flunked PE last year,* she reminded herself.

Yes, she was going to deal with Steve Mercer. And yes, she was going to do it alone. But she had to be smart. She had to have a plan. Tonight was not the night, no matter how much she wanted Mercer out of her life.

I'll just call the police and tell them there's a strange car in front of our house, Rae decided. *I won't even stick a toe outside.* She crept over to her window, wanting to confirm that someone was still in the driveway. Maybe she was getting all hysterical about someone who had only pulled in so they could turn around.

Rae pulled the curtain a few inches away from the edge of the window. A car was still in the driveway. Marcus's car.

Relief rushed through Rae, making her dizzy. *Guess I better go see what Mr. Salkow wants,* she thought. She was still dressed, so she was out of the house a few seconds later. Marcus climbed out of his Range Rover and cut across her front lawn to meet her.

"I wanted to give you this when it was still the actual day of Rae," Marcus said. "Happy birthday." He pulled a necklace out of his jacket pocket—no fancy jeweler's box this time, Rae noted.

"It's adorable," Rae said, touching the little beaded daisy at the end of the long, delicate chain.

"Really? You like it?" Marcus asked in full-out puppy dog mode.

"Really. I like it." Rae turned around. "Put it on me." She felt Marcus move up behind her, then heard him cursing softly as he struggled with the clasp. Finally the cool chain slid around her neck, and the daisy fell into place a few inches above the locket.

What a night, Rae thought. *What a hideous, beautiful, horrible, sad, amazing birthday night.* Marcus brushed against her as he began to step away. Without thinking about it, without analyzing or questioning, Rae turned around and hugged him, pressing her cheek against his chest.

Marcus didn't say a word. He just wrapped his arms around her and held on tight. Rae was sure if she could keep standing there forever, nothing bad would ever happen. Her body would never turn to lava the way it did when she was near Anthony, and a few days ago she thought she could never settle for less than that.

But it felt good snuggled next to Marcus. She felt a little like her old self, before her power had kicked in, before she'd met Anthony or Yana. She felt normal. And that felt nice.

I can have this, she thought. *I'll keep Marcus out of all the madness. He never has to know about Steve Mercer. He never has to know about my mom. He never has to know about my ability. We'll just be normal together. Rae and Marcus, Marcus and Rae, like we used to be. We'll go to the junior prom, and we'll—*

"So, does this mean—I'm hoping this means we're back together," Marcus whispered against her hair.

"Yes," Rae whispered. Yana could have Anthony. And Anthony could definitely have Yana. And Rae would have normal. No lava. But lots of sweet.

Marcus stepped back a half step, just enough so he could kiss her. *Mmm-hmm, very sweet,* Rae thought. *Happy birthday to me. This is just what I need.*

Anthony lay down in bed, then bolted upright again. Crap, he hadn't given Rae her birthday present. Not that it was anything so great, just one of those goofy little statues that said World's Best Teacher at the bottom. Because Rae *was* the best teacher he'd ever had. If she hadn't bullied him into letting her tutor him, he'd still be in the Bluebird trailer back at his old school.

He spotted a pair of sweatpants in the corner and pulled them on. They didn't smell so great, but who cared? He was just going to leave the present on her porch—with *from Anthony* written in really big letters so she didn't start thinking it was from the sicko who had sent her the ashes and the mutilated pictures.

Yeah, he thought as he pulled on a T-shirt. The porch plan was a good one. He didn't think Rae would want to see him right now. The look on her face when she'd realized that he was with Yana— man, it was like she'd ripped his heart out through his nostrils. He wanted to fall down in front of her and tell her that he knew he'd been an incredible flaming butt hole for not telling her what was going on with him and Yana. But before he could remember how to actually open his mouth, Rae was off to the bathroom. And when she came back, it was like nothing was wrong. Or at least like she was pretending nothing was wrong and she wanted everybody else to pretend, too. He figured Yana had explained the deal to her. Girls were better at that crap, anyway. But that didn't mean she'd want to see Anthony tonight. And besides, she was probably asleep.

And besides, you're a friggin' chicken, Anthony thought as he grabbed his keys and the present off the dresser and headed out of the house. Because deep down, since the second he'd seen that look on her face, something had been nagging away at him. And it wasn't just guilt for hurting her. It was the idea that it was possible that maybe Rae really didn't want to be with Marcus. Maybe she wanted . . .

Who knows what she wants, he thought as he got into the car and started driving toward Rae's. All he knew was that right now his brain couldn't handle actually coming right out and *thinking* whatever was down there in his gut. So it would just have to wait.

Anthony snapped on the radio to give his brain a break. About six songs later he turned onto Rae's street. He headed toward her house, starting to slow down. And then what he saw made him speed right back up, zooming by the Voight residence.

It's what you wanted, Anthony told himself as he turned toward home. *It's exactly what you friggin' wanted.* But right now, the image of Rae and Marcus on her front lawn, kissing, was making him so sick, he could barely drive.

Chapter 11

There are clocks everywhere in this school, Rae thought as she passed by one that had been incorporated into the mural of happy Sanderson prep graduates. Every time she looked at one of the clocks, her stomach got another knot, and her nerves stretched a little tighter. She had only three and a half hours before it was time to put her plan into action.

And before that? Not anything too stressful. Just lunch in the caf. With Marcus. As his girlfriend. *Pretend it's last spring, early last spring, before the meltdown,* Rae coached herself as she entered the cafeteria and got on the food line. *Pretend that it's the most normal thing in the world to go over to the table, sit down, and give Marcus a little kiss.* Well, maybe *normal* was the wrong word. It had never felt normal to Rae, even back then. It had felt magical, like somehow she'd entered a dreamworld where she was popular and completely accepted and so, so far from the dorky Rachel girl she'd been pre-seventh grade.

Rae paid for her veggie sandwich and iced tea, sucked in a deep breath, and made her way across the caf. Marcus was already at the table, smiling at her like, God, like there wasn't another girl anywhere in the world that he'd rather have coming toward him. But what about everybody else? Rae's eyes skittered away from Marcus to take in the rest of the group. Jackie was giving her an encouraging smile, like she got that this was hard for Rae. Vince was shoveling food in his mouth, oblivious to the minidrama. Lea, Lea, who became Rae's best friend practically the first day of the seventh grade, was going for casual but hadn't quite gotten there.

Maybe she's still afraid of me, Rae thought, remembering getting that horrible scrap of information from one of Lea's fingerprints at the beginning of the year. *If she is, she'll have to deal.* Rae stepped up to the table, put down her tray, and sat next to Marcus. She didn't have to worry about deciding whether or not to kiss him, since he immediately went for her lips, giving her a quick light kiss.

"Come on, you've got to give her some tongue," a guy called. Rae felt Marcus smile against her mouth, then he released her. The first thing she saw when she opened her eyes was Anthony Fascinelli. He was standing next to a grinning Chris McHugh, who'd definitely been the one coaching Marcus.

Rae kept her attention on Chris. She didn't think she could look at Anthony right now and keep up her here-I-am-sane-and-happy facade. "Chris, I'm going to have to give some serious thought to finding you a girlfriend," Rae told him.

Chris, his head looking like a big tomato, sat down next to Lea. Which left one seat open. The seat across from Rae. Anthony took it. Rae grabbed the pepper shaker, her fingers protected by wax, and shook some pepper onto her sandwich.

Got to remember to take the wax off right after school, Rae thought. Her plan didn't require using her fingerprint skills. But the plan, it might not go exactly the way she expected. She wanted to have any advantage she could get.

"It's good to see you guys back together," Jackie said to Rae and Marcus. Marcus wrapped his arm around Rae's waist and gave her a little squeeze. Rae slid a little closer to him, closer to his warmth. She wanted to soak up as much of it as she could before it was time to finally face down Steve Mercer. Rae's eyes went for the clock. *Hours and hours to go,* she thought. But hours and hours were nothing, really. By the end of the day her whole life would be different.

"Yeah, Marcus and Rae, together forever. How great is that?" Lea added. But it sounded like some of her vocal cords were made of cold metal instead of warm flesh. *She's not happy,* Rae realized. *She's not happy at all.*

Rae glanced over at Lea, and it was almost like looking at a stranger. *God, when you're a little girl, you really think the best-friend thing means something. It's so important. Who's your best friend? Are you your best friend's best friend? And where does that leave your other friend because you can't have two best friends?*

But the whole best-friend thing is crap. Lea couldn't take it when I snapped. Yana wouldn't even believe that I didn't send the letter. She didn't trust me even that much. And she didn't stop there. She decided to go after Anthony to make a point.

Rae's eyes moved to Anthony. She couldn't stop them. *Did you know why Yana was so hot to get together with you?* she silently asked. *Were you in it with her? Or was it much less complicated? Maybe if there's a chance to make out with a girl you think is cute, you go for it. Doesn't mean anything. Is that it, Anthony?*

Anthony met her gaze without looking away. She could see powerful emotion in the depths of his dark brown eyes. But what? Regret? Anger? What? *I don't know,* Rae realized. *I don't know him at all anymore.*

Rae snuggled even closer to Marcus. She knew what he was thinking. She knew what he wanted. He wanted to be with her as much as possible. Rae gave him a little kiss on the cheek, and he smiled.

"What are you doing tonight?" Marcus asked. "You want to get together, go for a ride or something?"

"Definitely," Rae answered. If her plan was successful, that's exactly what she'd want to do afterward. If her plan failed, then it didn't matter. Nothing mattered.

Anthony's feet felt like two big blocks of stone as he headed to the locker room. Usually football practice was the best part of the day. But at practice he'd have to see Marcus. And he knew if he looked at Marcus, it would trigger the memories in his brain. Marcus pulling Rae up against his side. Rae kissing Marcus on the cheek. Marcus kissing Rae on the mouth.

Crap, just thinking about seeing Marcus had gotten the memories playing. It was like getting punched in the gut over and over with his hands tied behind his back.

You wanted this to happen, Anthony reminded himself. And it was still what he wanted. He just didn't want to see it. Maybe he could poke his eyes out with a pencil or something.

"Wait up, Fascinelli," a voice called from behind him.

Anthony recognized the voice instantly. Friggin' Marcus Salkow.

Marcus trotted up and grabbed Anthony in a playful headlock. "Did you see it? Did you?" Anthony shoved Marcus away harder than he had to. Marcus didn't seem to notice. "Did you?" he repeated.

"See what?" Anthony asked, his head filled with images of Rae and Marcus. And somehow they were getting worse. He was seeing things he hadn't really seen.

"See me and Rae," Marcus answered. "She finally took me back."

Anthony rubbed the side of his head with his knuckles until it hurt so badly, the images disappeared. "Yeah, that's great. Way to go," he managed to say.

"It's thanks to you, you know that," Marcus told him. "You're the one who got me to stick it out, keep going back."

"I have to get something from my locker. See you in there," Anthony blurted when they reached the gym. He turned around and started to walk away fast.

"Okay, but just know that I know I owe you," Marcus called after him.

Anthony didn't look back. He strode into the first guys' bathroom he saw and slammed himself into a stall. *You are being such a freakin' girl,* he thought. *Hiding out in the bathroom.*

But he'd had to get away from Marcus. And he didn't want anybody looking at him. Because what if it showed on his face? What if it showed how—

Anthony refused to finish the thought. He slammed his fist into the side of the stall. Again, again. The flimsy wall was shaking. He knew that if it came down, he'd be in deep crap. But he didn't stop. It didn't hurt enough yet. It had to hurt more than it hurt to think about Rae and Marcus. Then he could stop.

Rae climbed out of the bus and crossed the street to the bank. At least the first stage of her plan was an easy one. She lingered on the front steps for a moment, pretending to look for something in her backpack but taking in the area with her peripheral vision. *You're watching me, Steve, aren't you?* she thought. *It's you in that blue Dodge parked across the street. I know it is. You've used that car to spy on me before.*

Okay, enough stalling. She wanted him to be able to keep track of her. But she didn't want him to know that. She hurried into the bank and over to one of the cluster of desks across from the long teller counter. "Hi," she said to the gray-haired man sitting there. "I was wondering if I could look at the safety deposit boxes. I'm thinking of getting one, and I just want to see what the system is."

"Want a safe place to keep the letters from your boyfriend?" the man teased, but not in a slimy way.

"Something like that," Rae answered. *I wish,* she thought. *I wish my life was what this guy imagines it is.*

"Come on. I'll give you the ten-cent tour," the man said as he stood up. "I'm Jimmy Baylis, by the way."

"Rae Voight." Rae followed Mr. Baylis to the back of the bank. He unlocked a door and ushered her into a room with what looked like dozens of metal drawers.

"Have a seat," Mr. Baylis told her. She sat down at the closest of the three long tables and clasped her hands in her lap. She didn't want anybody else's thoughts in her mind right now.

"Okay, here's what the boxes look like. Kind of like your own dresser drawer. Except smaller. And not in your dresser," Mr. Baylis said. He unlocked one of the boxes, slid it free, and set it down in front of Rae. "Plus much more secure."

"Looks good," Rae answered. "And there's, what, a monthly rental fee?" She didn't really care about the answer. But for the plan she needed to stay in here at least a few minutes. Enough time so that Steve Mercer would believe she'd taken something out of one of the boxes.

"Yearly," Mr. Baylis answered. "Except if you have a lot of money in an account." He winked at her. "Then it's free."

"And, um, there are other sizes?" Rae asked. Partly because she needed to be in here for the plan. But also, she had to admit, because she was afraid to go back out and do the rest of what she had to do.

"Other sizes, yes," Mr. Baylis told her. "Even a private booth you can go in when you open your box, if you don't want anybody to see what you've got stashed."

"Okay, well, that's it, I guess. Thanks," Rae answered, her voice coming out squeaky.

"My pleasure," Mr. Baylis said as he escorted her out.

Rae's knees trembled as she returned to the lobby

of the bank. It didn't seem like knees should be able to tremble. They were so hard, mostly bone, right? But hers were going like mad.

"On to phase two," Rae whispered. She pulled a large, lumpy manila envelope out of her backpack, then stepped back out into the sunlight. *I wore pink just so you'd have an easy time seeing me, you bastard,* Rae thought. In a leisurely way she walked back to the bus stop and was relieved to see the blue Dodge still parked across the street.

Plan's on track so far, she thought as she positioned herself next to the pole where the metal sign showing the bus routes was posted. She took an envelope out of her purse, slid out the birthday card inside, and opened it. She just wanted to make sure it said everything it needed to say.

Dear Steve,

I can call you Steve, can't I? Since you know me so well. Well, Steve, Saturday was my birthday. And I got a present from my dead mother. She thought maybe I'd get some powers kicking in around puberty, and she knew if I did, I'd be in danger. So she gave me a weapon—information to use against you. Something the police would love to see. Tissue samples can be kept for a

*long time, you know. And fingerprints? They
last for years and years.*

*I'm willing to give you the evidence—if
you agree to tell me everything about the
group and what exactly has given me the
powers I have. Oh, and one other thing. You
have to leave town forever.*

I'll be waiting at our motel.

> *Kisses,*
>
> *Rae*

That about says it all, Rae thought. Out of the corner of her eye she saw a few people stand up from the
bus stop bench. She checked the street. Yep, her bus
was coming. Quickly Rae replaced the card in the
envelope, then sealed it. She used a thick black Magic
Marker to write the name Steve Mercer in block letters on the front. When the bus pulled up to the stop,
Rae fished out the roll of tape in her purse and taped
the envelope to the metal pole, making sure that the
name was facing the direction of the Dodge.

The bus doors started to wheeze closed. "Wait,
I'm coming," Rae cried. The doors reopened, and
Rae climbed on. *He's got to see the envelope,* she
thought. *It's practically taped to his windshield.
He'll take the bait. I know it.*

*   *   *

Rae double-checked the duct tape holding the little tape recorder to the underside of the nightstand in room 212 of the Motel 6, her home away from home. Then she pushed the record button, getting a fragment of one of her own frightened thoughts. Like she didn't have enough of them slamming around in her head already. *An hour of tape,* she thought. *It'll be plenty. This whole thing is going to be settled one way or the other in less than an hour.*

Okay, camera, camera. Rae's video camera wasn't huge or anything. But it definitely wasn't a tiny, super-high-tech one. She scanned the room. Not many good places to hide it. *Hurry. Got to hurry. He could be here any second.* The thought got Rae moving. She rushed over to the window and strapped the video camera to the side of the window frame, getting thoughts that felt like echoes since she was still having them.

/What if/Dad will never/Mercer's killed/Don't know/God/

It looks so obvious, Rae thought. But it was too late to find a better spot. She arranged the curtain around the camera in what she prayed looked like a natural drape, then taped the curtain in place. "Shut up," she muttered as her old thoughts flickered through her mind. She backed away from the window and sat down on the very edge of the bed.

Maybe he'll be distracted, she thought. *And even if he finds the camera, there's still the—*

A quiet knock jerked her out of her thoughts. He was here. She stood up and walked to the door, her knees trembling so hard, they were sending shudders all the way down her legs. Rae checked the peephole. She wasn't completely surprised by who she saw, but she still felt her heart pound just a little harder. It was the guy who'd posed as the meter reader in her backyard. She'd been standing that close to the man who killed her mother, in her own yard, and she hadn't had a clue. Now he was wearing a suit and tie, and he looked about as scary as Mr. Baylis from the bank. And just about as calm. As if this was no big deal at all.

Time for the final phase of the plan, Rae thought. She swung open the door and backed into the center of the room. "Start talking," Rae blurted. "Start talking, and when I've heard everything I want to hear, I'll take you to the evidence. It's in a safe place. But you'll never find it without me."

Mercer slowly shut the door behind him. He walked into the room, toward Rae, then pulled out the chair in front of the table across from the bed and sat down. Then he looked at Rae. Just looked at her, waiting to see what she'd do next but not all that worried about it.

And why would he be? Rae thought, hysteria surging inside her. *Remember how many people he's killed? And you expect him to be afraid of you.*

The evidence, she reminded herself. *You have the evidence.* Of course, she didn't really have the evidence. There was no evidence. But she couldn't let him suspect that, or she'd never leave this room alive.

"If we don't get to the place I stashed it in half an hour, I made arrangements for someone to pick it up," Rae lied. God, maybe she should have said fifteen minutes. Ten minutes. Five minutes, even. But she wanted him to have the time to tell her everything. "Start with what you did to my mother."

"I understand that you're angry. But I'm not the person you're looking for," Mercer said. He propped one foot on the opposite knee.

"You're telling me you didn't kill my mother?" Rae burst out. She hadn't meant to say that. She'd wanted him to volunteer the information all on his own, so it wouldn't seem like she was putting words in his mouth on the tape. Well, forget it. Nothing she could do about it now.

Mercer rubbed his left temple with his knuckles. "Oh, I killed her," he answered.

Rae sank down on the edge of the bed. If she didn't, she knew she'd end up on the floor. Her legs weren't strong enough to hold her anymore. He admitted it. Just like that. So calm. So rational. So cold. He'd said it in a tone someone would use to admit to leaving the toilet seat up or forgetting to lock a door. It was nothing, no big deal. Rae struggled not to lunge at the man and strangle him with her bare hands. But she needed to hear the rest—she needed to hear all of it.

"I had no choice," he continued. "The good of the many outweighs the good of the one or the few. You're a smart girl. You must understand that."

"Are you even human?" Rae got out through clenched teeth. Then she forced herself to remember what she wanted. A confession. On tape. "Can you tell me how you did it? I . . . I think about it all the time. Was she in pain? I need to know. Please." Rae wanted her voice to come out trembly and vulnerable sounding, and that was no problem.

"The virus I gave her acted very quickly. And I'm sure her doctors kept her very comfortable," Mercer answered. Then he smiled at her, actually smiled. "Morphine, I'd imagine. You don't have to think of her in pain."

No, I just have to think of her dead, Rae thought. *He's insane. He really is insane, sitting over there, smiling at me, as if he actually cares about reassuring me.*

"You said you're not who I'm looking for," she said carefully. "But you killed her. So I don't get it—who am I looking for, then?"

"I wasn't talking about looking for anyone," Mercer said. "I meant that I'm not responsible for your mother's death. The woman who ordered the experiments is. I didn't know she was government. I didn't know what she really wanted. I never would have had to take the action I took if it wasn't for the way she used me for her own agenda."

"Did she order you to kill my mother, too? Did she order you to kill Amanda Reese?" Rae demanded.

Mercer's eyes opened a fraction wider, but they could still be sitting there talking about quilting or a math problem if you went by the way he was acting. "No, I did that on my own," Mercer answered. "I had to. No one else would take responsibility. Do you know what happens in a world where no one takes responsibility?"

His voice had gotten louder, and his breathing had sped up. Rae could hear his fast, ragged breaths from her seat on the bed.

"I'll tell you what happens," Mercer rushed on. "Chaos." He gave his head a violent shake. "The experiments changed them. It changed them all. But I didn't kill them. Not until I saw a sign. I just watched.

Watched and documented. And when I saw a sign, then I took responsibility."

"Then you murdered them," Rae said softly. Beads of sweat had popped out on Mercer's forehead, but Rae felt cold, cold deep in the marrow of her bones.

"Yes!" Mercer exclaimed. He jumped out of his chair and began to pace. "I. Took. Responsibility. I went to the mental hospital where your mother was held. I dressed as an orderly. It was easy. I had the syringe with the virus in my pocket. I walked in. Injected the virus into her IV. Walked out."

Ice formed around Rae's internal organs. Each breath was an effort. Her lungs had to break the ice to expand, to get oxygen. But the moment the air was released, Rae could feel the ice re-forming.

"She was dangerous, Rae. She had to die. It was better for you that she did," Mercer rushed on, pacing faster and faster. Abruptly he stopped directly in front of Rae. "I was hoping the next generation wouldn't be infected. But it was. You know that. Still I waited. Hoping that a sign wouldn't come. That some kind of mutation had occurred that would make the G-2s benign. But when you had your breakdown in the spring, it was the sign I hoped I wouldn't see. Your behavior today confirms that my fears about you were correct."

He leaned down, so close, Rae could feel his hot,

fast breaths against her face. She struggled to pull in a breath of her own. The shards of ice jabbed into her expanding lungs, sending spears of pain into Rae.

"I never wanted to kill you, Rae. But I must take responsibility." Rae's breath froze in her chest as Mercer pulled on a pair of thin rubber gloves, then removed a gun from the inside pocket of his jacket. He pried open her jaw and slid the metal barrel between her teeth.

It singed the cold flesh of her mouth. *What should I do? What am I supposed to do?* Rae thought. But there was nothing to do. She had a gun in her mouth. Her only option was to stay motionless and . . . and . . .

Mercer wrapped Rae's fingers around the barrel of the gun. She didn't pick up a single thought. The only fingerprints would be her own.

"Teen suicide is such a tragedy," Mercer said as he moved her trigger finger into place.

"The evidence," Rae managed to say around the gun. "Evidence," she repeated when he just stared at her blankly.

"The evidence will show that what I did, I did for humanity," Mercer answered. He sounded calm again. Calm and determined.

I'm going to die, Rae thought. *My dad . . .*

The motel door flew open. Mercer jerked toward

the sound. Rae wrestled the gun out of her mouth and flung it across the room, the metal taste like poison against her tongue.

"Both of you stay where you are," a man ordered. Rae's gaze snapped to the voice. Three men were lined up just inside the doorway. There were more in the hall. All wore masks. And all carried guns, sleek high-tech things.

"Who—" Rae said. Before she could get out another word, Mercer jerked her to her feet and pinned her against him. A shield. He was using her as a shield.

All three men had their guns aimed at Mercer. Mercer and so Rae. "Put them down or you'll end up killing her," Mercer told them.

Rae felt a rush of air over the top of her head. Then Mercer went down, bringing her with him. Rae knew before she looked that he was dead. She scrambled to her feet and stared down at him. His eyes stared blankly up at hers, the small bullet hole like a third eye in the center of his forehead.

They could have killed me, Rae thought as she turned to face the men. *And they didn't even care. Are they going to shoot me, too?* The thoughts moved slowly through her cold, numb brain. She didn't step away as one of the men moved toward her. He pulled out a pair of handcuffs.

"No!" one of the men in the hall barked. The man

with the handcuffs took a step away. The man who'd yelled from the hall strode up to Rae. "If you leave now and make no further attempts to get information on the group, you will be allowed to live."

Rae recognized the voice. It was Aiden standing in front of her.

"Don't think that we won't know. You will be watched. And you will be killed immediately if you don't do as I say."

Rae nodded. She made her way to the door on the sticks of ice that were her legs. *Already found the hiding place for my tape recorder,* she thought dully as she saw one of the men reach for it out of the corner of her eye. *They'll have the camera in another second.*

"Leave it alone, Rae," Aiden called after her. "It's over now."

Over now, Rae repeated to herself as she stepped out of the room. The men in the hall moved aside just enough to let her pass.

One of them will follow me home, she realized. *One of them will follow me everywhere from now on.*

She walked down the hall on her cold, numb feet. *Over now. That's what I thought. I thought that after today, it would be over—one way or the other. But no matter what Aiden says, it's not over. It's never going to be over.*

turn the page
for a preview of
fingerprints #6:

revelations

Chapter 1

Okay, *you can do this*, Rae Voight thought. *You have to do this.* She peered down the hallway she knew Anthony would use to get to the cafeteria. She didn't want to see Anthony. Not now. Not ever. Which was why she'd been avoiding him for days. But she had to talk to him. He had a right to know how things had ended. Until she told him, she couldn't get on with her life. And that's all she wanted. To get on with her normal-girl life with her so-far-above-normal-former-ex-boyfriend Marcus Salkow.

Thinking of Marcus made her feel all cozy, like she'd been wrapped in her favorite fuzzy blanket. *A few minutes with Anthony, then it can be all Marcus all the time,* Rae promised herself. She took another look down the hall. *Come on, Anthony, come on,* she thought. *I want to get this over with.*

An electric tingle ran down Rae's spine. And a moment later she saw Anthony heading toward her. It was like the rest of her body recognized him before her eyes did. Except no. No. There was no reason for a surge of energy to run through her just because Anthony Fascinelli was in the vicinity.

Rae nervously fluffed her curly, reddish brown hair. She wished she'd worn shoes with higher heels. It would feel good to be taller than Anthony during this conversation. Maybe she should wait until tomorrow and—

No, Rae ordered herself. *You are doing this. Right here. Right now.* "Anthony," she called out before she could change her mind. He reached her way too quickly. She wasn't ready. She—

"Steve Mercer is dead," she blurted. "So no one's after me anymore. I just wanted you to know because . . . because in a way he was after you, too, since you were helping me. So thanks. And have a nice life."

Anthony blinked. "Back up," he demanded, staring at her as if she were speaking another language. "*Who* is Steve Mercer?"

Like you care, Rae wanted to scream at him. Instead she pulled in a long, slow breath. Somehow it had all blurred together in her mind . . . what Anthony knew and what he didn't know. Maybe because she was trying her hardest not to know any of it anymore, to just forget it had ever happened.

"Steve Mercer was a scientist," she explained. "He was in charge of that group my mother was in."

"Right. The group," Anthony agreed. He paused. "Hold on—a scientist? I don't get it. What exactly was the group about?"

Rae swallowed. Why couldn't Anthony just let her get through this quickly?

"The group was—they were people who had some kind of special ability," she said. She glanced around the hallway almost out of habit, then reminded herself that no one was after her anymore. "And Mercer's job was to get the people in the group to develop major psi powers," she continued, focusing her gaze back on Anthony. "Drugs, radiation, shock treatment—you name it, Steve did it to them. To my mom," she added in a softer voice.

"And it worked," Anthony said, his brown eyes wide in amazement.

"Yeah, it worked so well that I ended up . . . you know," Rae said. "And that's why Mercer was after me. I guess the guy went kind of nuts. He decided that what he'd done to the members of the group was dangerous to society. So he basically went on a little killing spree. He killed my mom and at least one other person from the group. Maybe more. And he watched the kids who were born after the experiment. Watched us our whole lives. When he saw that I had been affected, he decided he needed to kill me, too."

Rae shook her head hard. "But you don't need to know all this. What you need to know is that it's over. Mercer's dead. Guys from the government agency that funded the experiments killed him. So no one's going to be attempting to massacre me again. No one's going to get kidnapped."

"That's great. That's so freakin' great." Anthony reached for her. Rae jumped away, scraping her back against the corner of the trophy case behind her. How could he even think of touching her after what he'd done to her?

"Freakin' great," Rae repeated. "Yeah. Exactly. So what I wanted to tell you is your life can go back to normal. Yours and Yana's." The name Yana felt like it was made of razor blades. Rae was surprised her mouth didn't start bleeding the second she'd gotten the name out.

"Rae . . . I . . ." Anthony jammed his hands into his pockets. "I should have told you that Yana and I had hooked up. I shouldn't have—"

"What?" Rae interrupted. "Shouldn't have destroyed my little sweet-sixteen birthday dinner by showing up with Yana?"

"It's not like you and I were ever—" Anthony began to protest.

"I thought we were friends," Rae interrupted. "That's what I thought we were. And then you get together with Yana just so I'd know how it felt to have someone go behind my back. Even though I only looked for your dad because I wanted to help, and I didn't even send Yana's dad that stupid letter."

"The letter about treating Yana better? What does that have to do with—"

"Yes, that letter. Don't bother pretending to be so innocent, Anthony," Rae cut in again. "I know you and Yana got together as payback. She *told* me. She thought I went behind her back with the letter, so she decided to go behind mine. And you went along for the ride."

"You just assume I was in on it, right?" Anthony said, his voice flat. "You don't even ask me. You just assume. Because that's just the kind of thing I'd do."

"So you started going out with my best friend because you—" Rae began.

This time Anthony interrupted her. "Because she's hot, okay? And it's not like you and I were—"

"But you kissed me," Rae accused. "And then you were sticking your tongue down Yana's throat two seconds later." She pressed the heels of her hands against her forehead, then dropped her arms to

5

her sides. "This isn't what I wanted to say to you. I just wanted you to know that everything is over and that you, Jesse, me, we're all safe."

Rae forced herself to meet Anthony's gaze. Usually his eyes reminded her of melted Hershey's Kisses. But right now they were hard and cold. "Thanks. Thanks for what you did for me."

"Yeah, thanks, and now that you have no use for me, I should just get away from you, right, Rae?"

"It was your choice," she muttered. Then she had to look away. She felt like Anthony's eyes were turning her to ice. "Oh, there's Marcus. I should go." She didn't wait for an answer. She just rushed over to Marcus and hurled herself at him, wrapping her arms around his neck.

"Hi," Marcus mumbled against her lips.

Rae didn't answer. She closed her eyes, wanting to lose herself in the taste of Marcus. Just kiss him and kiss him and kiss him.

"Maybe we should take this to my car," Marcus finally said, pulling away half an inch.

"Maybe," Rae agreed. She slid her arm around his waist, turned him toward the nearest exit—and saw Mr. Jesperson staring at them. The teacher creeped her out, always so interested in how she was *doing,* but Rae forced herself to smile at him, anyway. *Look at me, Mr. Jesperson,* she thought. *I'm fine. I'm more than fine. You don't have to worry about poor, troubled Rae Voight anymore. I have my life back. And I'm going to make it perfect. Perfect with Marcus.*

"I know we're going to the car," Rae told Marcus. "But I think I have to kiss you again right here."

Anthony felt his lips heat up. Like he was the one kissing Rae instead of Marcus. *But you're not,* he told himself. *She made it glass clear that you're dead as far as she's concerned. Dead and rotting.*

Saliva flooded his mouth, and he got that about-to-puke feeling. He had to get out of there. Anthony turned on his heel and strode back down the hall and out into the parking lot. He pulled in gulps of the crisp fall air until his stomach stopped trying to jerk itself up his throat, then he headed over to his car—technically his mom's car—and got in. He put the Hyundai in reverse and backed out of the parking lot so fast that the motion threw his body forward. He didn't care. He had to get out of there. Away from Rae. Rae and Marcus and kissing. Now, now, now.

Anthony just drove. He didn't care where he was going as long as it was away. At least that's what he thought until he realized he was heading to Yana's school. He did a cop check of the street, then pressed the gas pedal down a little farther. Less than two minutes later he was parked in front of the school. He didn't want to waste time looking for her, so he asked the security guard at the closest entrance where to find the main office. After the guy did a friggin' inspection of Anthony's ID, he pointed Anthony down a hallway to the left. Anthony held himself to a walk, even though he wanted to put down his head and plow the way he did on the football field.

"I'm Yana Savari's cousin," he announced as soon as he was through the office door. "There's a family emergency. I'm supposed to get Yana and take her to the hospital."

Anthony expected to get a bunch of questions, but the girl behind the desk, who didn't look any older than he was, didn't seem to care. She just turned to the computer, hit a few keys, then said, "Room 104. You want to go down there and get her yourself?"

"Yeah. Thanks," Anthony answered, already halfway out the door.

"You take a right, then another right," the girl called after him. Anthony allowed himself to trot down the hall, not run, since running could get him stopped by a random teacher wandering the halls. His sneakers squeaked as he made the second right. He swung his head back and forth as he started down the hall. Room 104. Yeah. Anthony veered over to it, gave a light little knock, then opened the door and leaned inside.

He blurted his cover story to the teacher. She

looked dubious, but when he said he'd already been to the office, she let Yana go. Anthony focused his gaze a little to Yana's left as she crossed the room toward him. He couldn't really look at her. If he did, he wasn't sure he'd be able to stop himself from ripping her lying head right off her neck.

Anthony pressed himself against the door frame as Yana walked past him, but her body still brushed against his. The contact got his stomach heaving again. He gave a couple of hard swallows, then, when he was sure he wasn't going to spew right there, he stepped out into the hall after Yana and closed the door behind him.

"You must be psychic or something," Yana told him. "I need to talk to you so badly. My father is—"

"Shut up," Anthony ordered. "I don't want to hear anything out of you. The only reason I'm here is to tell you that I don't want you within one hundred feet of me ever."

"I'm trying to tell you that—" Yana protested.

"Yeah. I want to hear more of your lies," Anthony cut her off.

Yana's blue eyes became electric, all the vulnerability from a second ago gone. Anthony could almost feel them crackling. "More lies? Exactly what lies have I supposedly told you?"

"Um. Hmmm. What was it?" Anthony snapped. "Oh, yeah. You were using me to get back at Rae for that letter she supposedly sent to your dad. And that makes pretty much everything you've said to me since we started hooking up a lie."

"Oh, and it was so awful for you, wasn't it?" Yana shot back. "Making out with me for hours at a time."

"I'm done with you," Anthony told her. There was no point in having some long, drawn-out conversation about it all. He turned away from Yana and started down the hall away from her. A second later she grabbed his elbow, her grip a lot stronger than he'd expected it to be. She yanked him around to face her.

"Listen, jerk, I had fun with you, okay?" Yana said, not letting go of his arm. "It wasn't just about giving Rae a lesson in how it feels to be backstabbed. I mean, yeah, that was why I started up the thing with you. But I . . . I liked it, you know. And you seemed to be having a pretty good time yourself."

Anthony ripped his arm away from Yana's grip. "Yeah, I had a good time. Because I was a freakin' moron. I didn't even think about the possibility that—" Anthony shook his head. "This is a waste. I've already said what I came for—to tell you to stay far away from me." He turned and started down the hall again. Nothing she could say, nothing she could do, was going to change his mind. He never wanted to see her lying face again.

*   *   *

Rae ran the tiny brush over the nail of her index finger, enjoying the faint coolness of the polish. And the beauty of its wet mauveness. She giggled. She couldn't believe that she was marveling over finger-nail polish, like it was so wonderful, it was proof of God's existence.

She couldn't help it, though. Everything felt . . . more precious now, now that her life was her own again. The sensation of her freshly shaved legs brush-ing against the inside of her khakis was delicious. The splotches of sunlight on her bedroom floor made her want to curl up inside one of them. The sound of her Radiohead CD was vibrating in her bones, and it felt like the music was coming out of her instead of some-thing she was just passively listening to.

I have to hold on to this, Rae thought. *I don't want to ever forget how amazing it is just to be alive.* She began to paint the next naked fingernail. Then the phone rang.

It's Anthony, she thought. *You don't know that,* she corrected herself. *It could be Marcus. It's much more likely that it's Marcus. Marcus is your boyfriend. Marcus is the one taking you to the dance tonight.* Rae gingerly picked up the phone, careful not to do any damage to her wet nails. "Hello."

"Hi, Rae. This is Ms. Abramson."

Oh, goody, my therapist, Rae thought. But a call

from Ms. Abramson wasn't enough to shake her out of her glorious mood. Not nearly enough.

"I know we have an individual appointment after the next group session," Ms. Abramson continued, "but I was wondering if we could push it back a few days."

"Yeah, that works for me," Rae answered. "Except I don't know if I really need an individual session. I don't think I need therapy at all anymore. Everything is going so great. I even got back with my old boyfriend. I'm feeling incredible."

"I'm glad to hear it," Ms. Abramson answered. "But ending therapy is a big decision, and it's not something that should be done abruptly. Look, why don't we do an individual appointment after the last group session of this week? We can talk about a strategy for tapering off therapy if we both decide that's what's best for you. How does that sound?"

"Fine," Rae answered. What else could she say? She should have known Ms. Abramson wouldn't just be like, "Wonderful, Rae. You never have to come to therapy again. Have a fabulous life."

"All right. See you in group," Ms. Abramson said.

"Okay. Bye." Rae gently hung up the phone. The mauve of her nail polish didn't seem quite so amazing anymore. *Think about the dance,* Rae ordered herself. *Think about you and Anthony there. Marcus!*

she corrected herself. *You and Marcus. Dancing. Him holding you close.*

God, it was probably the dream of every girl in school. And it was Rae's life. She couldn't believe Anthony's name had popped into her head like that. *It's just because you had to deal with him today,* she told herself. *But you did it. You told him what you needed to tell him, and you don't ever have to talk to him again.*

The doorbell rang, pulling Rae out of her thoughts. "It's Anthony," she murmured. She could almost see him out on the porch, wanting a chance to explain to her again that he didn't know what Yana had planned. *But it doesn't matter whether he knew or not,* Rae told herself. *He still went sneaking around with her. He could have told me, but—*

The doorbell rang again. Rae stood up, glad she hadn't started painting her toenails yet, and hurried to the door. She pulled it open. Her first instinct was to slam it shut. Because Yana was standing there.

As if Yana expected Rae to do just that, she reached out and held the door open with one hand. "I know you hate me right now," she said, and her voice came out all trembly.

"Yeah, I do," Rae told her. She gave the door a shove, but Yana's hand held it open.

"I know. I know. But I need your help, Rae. I really need your help," Yana blurted.

She's been crying, Rae realized, taking in Yana's bloodshot eyes and puffy face. Rae had never seen Yana even close to this upset. *But that's not my problem.* "We're not friends," Rae said. "You can't trust me, remember? You're so sure I went behind your back and sent your dad that letter. I'm the last person you should be coming to. Why don't you go find one of your real friends?"

"You are my friend. My only real friend," Yana said, her voice getting higher with each word.

God, she's about to snap, Rae realized.

"I wouldn't have come here if I wasn't desperate," Yana continued. "I know you don't want to see me. But you're the only one who can help me, Rae. The only one. I need you to use your power."

* * *

I can't stand to think about Rae right now. She's so happy. So sure the world is a wonderful place created just for her. So excited about having her perfect boyfriend back.

It makes me sick. Rae doesn't deserve a happy life. She doesn't deserve a life at all. And I'm going to make sure she doesn't have one for long. But before I kill her, I think Rae should be forced to remember that the world isn't her own private toy. I don't want her to die when she's this happy. That's not the revenge that I deserve. I want her to feel all the pain I've been forced to feel. When she has, then it will be time for her to die.

14

**Turn the page for a
sneak peek at another great
series from HarperCollins:**

The Black Book
[DIARY OF A TEENAGE STUD]

---■---

I'm lying in bed writing by the light of my crappy bedside lamp. It's after one in the morning. Posie was just here. The whole room still smells like her—like saltwater and sunscreen.

I was finishing my German homework when I heard a boat out on the canal and a light drawing up to the dock and two seconds later there she is, knocking on the glass. I love the way she just shows up.

Her hair was wet and she had this big grin on her face. "Can I come in?" she said.

I slid open the door and she came in. She was wearing the top half of a red string bikini and that purple sarong skirt I'd seen her wear before and no shoes. I stopped for a second, just taking her in.

"Jeez, Jonah, stop staring at my boobs," she

1

said, but she didn't sound mad. She just stood there watching me drink her up.

"I hope you don't mind me coming over," she said. "I was out night-surfing. It was so completely gnarly, I couldn't see a thing. How are you doing, anyway?"

"I'm all right," I said.

"Hey, do you mind if I sit down on your bed? I'm still a little wet from surfing."

I moved my books out of the way, and she sat down and leaned her back against the wall. She looked around my room.

"I've missed having you around, Jonah. You're the only person in the universe I can talk to," she said.

"What about Thorne? He didn't go anywhere," I said.

"Oh, well, Thorne is a sweetheart, but you know what he's like. All he wants to do is talk about sex all the time. It kind of wears me down after a while, to tell you the truth."

I liked that Posie said that. I wanted to be the one she talked to. But what about Wailer? What was she going out with him for if she couldn't talk to him? I didn't say anything, though. I didn't want to piss her off, and I really didn't want her to leave. She might be my best friend, but I couldn't help staring at the way the salt had crusted on her eye-lashes, like crystals. In the hollows of her collar-bone, too. She looked like a mermaid.

"You want a chaw?" Posie asked, and I snapped out of it. I don't think she caught me looking. Or if she did, she didn't mind.

"No, thanks. But you go ahead," I said.

She filled her cheek with chewing tobacco, then reached down her bikini top and scratched under her breasts. It seems like she is always scratching them in front of me. I guess it's nice that Posie feels comfortable around me.

"This top is murder. You don't have a T-shirt I could borrow, do you?" she asked.

I walked over to my dresser and got a plain white T-shirt from the second drawer and tossed it to her. Posie stood up, turned her back to me, and picked at the back of her bikini.

"Damn. Can you untie this thing for me?"

"Sure." I worked at the knot, which was hard to undo because it was wet, and my hands were sort of trembling. When it came loose Posie let the top fall onto the floor and for just a second I saw her bare back. I think a girl's bare back has got to be the most incredible thing in the world. I mean, part of it is just the drama of knowing how cool it would be if they turned around. But their backs also look so delicate and vulnerable you just want to touch them. Posie's does, anyway.

Posie pulled my shirt over her head and turned around and sat back down on the bed. My shirt definitely looked better on her than on me.

"That's better," she said. One of her cheeks was full of tobacco. She looked like Popeye the Sailor Man. "So what's the story with the girl in Pennsylvania? Are you two still seeing each other?"

"Sophie," I said. "You mean Sophie?"

"Yeah. What's up with her?" Posie said.

I felt my ears getting hot. I didn't know what to tell her.

Posie looked at me and poked me in the arm. "Jonah. You're shaking," she said.

"Um, I d-don't know what to say," I stuttered. "We kind of had a misunderstanding."

Posie stood up and spat a big squirt of juice out the window into my mother's shrubs. Then she sat down next to me on the bed.

"Jonah, babe, it sounds like you really loved her," she said.

"I think I did, Posie," I said. "I think I'm a little messed up now."

My voice choked a little, and Posie gave me this great big hug. It felt great, the best feeling I've had since I came back.

4

"You know what you need, Jonah? You need . . . excuse me." She went to the window again and spat out another big squirt of juice. "You need a woman."

"Yeah, well, Thorne has me all lined up with his ex-girlfriends," I said.

"That's not what I mean. I mean somebody of your own," Posie said. She looked at her watch. "Oh, my God, it's almost one in the morning. I've got to go."

She slid open the glass door and blew the rest of the tobacco juice out into my mother's hydrangeas. "Don't worry, Jonah. We'll work it out," she said, turning back to me. Then she came back over to the bed and gave me another big hug and kissed me on the lips.

"You'd better not have a boner, or I'm going to punch your lights out," she said.

"I'm fine. Believe me. I hardly even notice you're a girl," I said. It's funny. I didn't used to notice Posie was a girl, but I do now. It's painful.

"I'm a girl?" Posie said, in shock, and looked down at her chest. "Oh, my God! You're right!"

Then she ran outside, and a second later I heard her boat roar on up the creek.

I looked at the place where she'd been sitting on the bed. There were two wet butt cheek marks on my sheets.

Then I looked down at the floor. She'd left her bikini top behind.

My bedroom door creaked open and my sister poked her head into the room.

"Can I come in here, Lamo, or are you jerking off?" Honey said.

"Come on in," I said.

Honey opened the door. She was wearing a black T-shirt with a skull on it that said HARLEY-DAVIDSON.

"So. Who's your friend?" she asked me.

"I don't know what you're talking about," I said, trying to be mysterious.

"You're telling me some girl didn't just spit tobacco juice out your window?"

"A girl? No," I said.

Honey walked into the room and picked Posie's bikini top up off the floor. She held it up.

"This is really cute," she said. "You'll definitely look hot in this."

"It's Posie's," I said, bored with our little game. "She stopped in on her way back from surfing."

"She's loaning you her stuff now?" Honey said. "Man, that's open-minded."

She examined Posie's bikini top carefully and whistled.

"Up yours," I said.

"Hey, you want to borrow any of my undies? You want to start wearing girls' panties to school every day, you just say the word."

"Did you want something, or did you just come in here to annoy me?" I said.

"Listen, Phlegmball, can I ask you a question?" Honey said.

"Anything for you," I said.

"What's that chick like, that Dad married?" Honey said.

I was surprised. Honey always acts so tough. After Dad moved out, she pretty much pretended she forgot about him.

"Tiffany? I don't know. She's young, I guess. You'd say she's young," I said.

"Like what? Six, seven years old?" Honey said.

"I think she's twenty-three."

"His secretary," she said.

"His former secretary," I corrected her. I was watching Honey's face to see how this information was affecting her, but she seemed unmoved.

"And so what, he like, buys her horses, jewelry, that kind of thing?" she said.

"Yeah. Well, they're married and all."

Honey stood there looking at her nails. Some of them were pretty long. She had this kind of blank expression.

7

———— ∎ ————

"You think he's gonna call me on my birthday?" she asked me.

"Sure, he will," I said, although I wasn't at all sure. Dad's not exactly the most thoughtful person in the world.

"Well, he can call or he can not call. I don't give a crap," Honey said.

"You could call *him*," I said.

"Yeah. Right. Hey listen, is there anything I can do for you, Spazmo? Is there anything you want? Cuban cigars? The answers to the SAT? What?"

I noticed she was changing the subject, but that was all right. There was something I wanted. Badly.

"I want to be a senior," I told her.

"A senior? You mean like, you need me to break into the master record room, forge a bunch of documents from Masthead, alter your transcript, that kind of thing?"

"Yeah," I said hopefully. "Could you do that? I mean, seriously? Could you?"

"You mean like could I get my hacker friends to crack the school's computer, and make the changes?" she said.

"Yes," I said, getting excited. "Can you do that? Please?"

She shrugged. "Sorry, Nutly. I can't hack into the school's computer."

———■———

"How do you know if you haven't tried?"

Honey smiled. "You think I haven't tried?"

She went to the door. "If you change your mind about the panties thing, though, let me know."

Then she walked back to her room, and I crawled into bed and wrote this. Now I'm going to sleep.